Special thanks to Michael Ford

ORCHARD BOOKS

First published in Great Britain in 2023 by Hodder & Stoughton

1 3 5 7 9 10 8 6 4 2

Text © Beast Quest Limited 2023
Cover and inside illustrations by Martin Bustamante
© Beast Quest Limited 2023

Series created by Beast Quest Limited, London

A CIP catalogue record for this book is available from the British Library.

ISBN 978 1 40836 372 0

Printed in Great Britain

The paper and board used in this book are made from wood from responsible sources

Orchard Books
An imprint of Hachette Children's Group
Part of Hodder & Stoughton Limited
Carmelite House, 50 Victoria Embankment, London EC4Y 0DZ

An Hachette UK Company
www.hachette.co.uk
www.hachettechildrens.co.uk

BEASTHEART

CONJUROR

A.H. BLADE

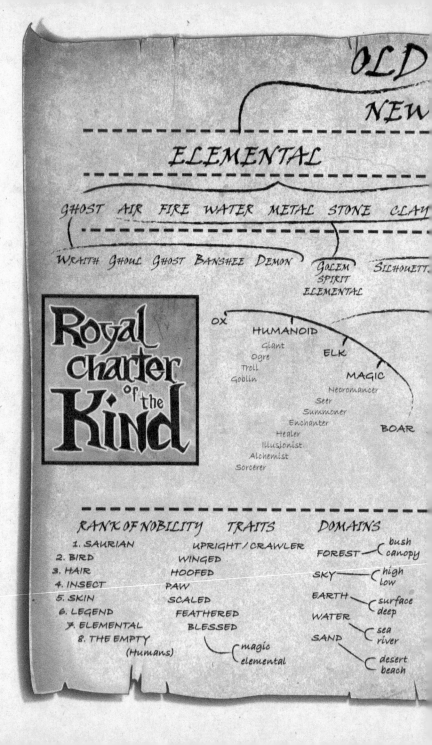

OLD

NEW

ELEMENTAL

GHOST   AIR   FIRE   WATER   METAL   STONE   CLAY

WRAITH   GHOUL   GHOST   BANSHEE   DEMON   GOLEM   SILHOUETT.
SPIRIT
ELEMENTAL

OX

HUMANOID
Giant
Ogre   ELK
Troll
Goblin   MAGIC
Necromancer
Seer
Summoner
Enchanter   BOAR
Healer
Illusionist
Alchemist
Sorcerer

RANK OF NOBILITY   TRAITS   DOMAINS
1. SAURIAN   UPRIGHT / CRAWLER   ┌ bush
2. BIRD   WINGED   FOREST ─┤ canopy
3. HAIR   HOOFED   SKY ──────┤ high
4. INSECT   PAW   └ low
5. SKIN   SCALED   EARTH ─┤ surface
6. LEGEND   FEATHERED   └ deep
7. ELEMENTAL   BLESSED   WATER ─┤ sea
8. THE EMPTY   └ river
   (Humans)   ┌ magic   SAND ─┤ desert
                         └ elemental   └ beach

KIND

KIND

| | TRUE | ORIGIN |

| | BIRTH |

HADOW PLANT LIVE EGG

REAM SKIN HAIR

SAURIAN BIRD INSECT | KIND and SUB-KIND

MAMMOTH

CAT
Tiger
Lion
Lynx
Leopard
Panther

EAR

HOUND
Wolf
Dog

HAWK
Phoenix
Eagle
Vulture

SPIDER
Spider
Scorpion
Ant
Wasp

LIZARD
Lesser Dragon
Wyvern
Salamander
Gecko
Komodo
Chameleon

SNAKE
Wyrm
Basilisk
Hydra
Python

LEGEND-KIND

Lesser Dragon
Lesser Phoenix
Lesser Hydra
Lesser Centaurs
Lesser Griffins
Lesser Minotaurs,
Ogres, Giants, Trolls

by order of

Malachai

First of the Learned Kind
Year 503 after Spawning

THE CHRONICLES OF HAVANTHYA

Havanthya is falling. Balance is gone from the world. Civil war ravages the land. Though many have claimed to be Masters of the Kind in the fifty years since Thom's death, these pretenders seek only power. As the Kind are driven from their lands and slain, the so-called Masters do nothing to save these mighty creatures.

So few remain.

The phoenix Aephos; Sephron the sea serpent; Caymer the hound – all slaughtered. The twin dragons Krimios and Vedrios were meant to usher in a new era of peace, but poor Krimios was butchered.

These creatures had devoted their lives to helping mankind keep peace and balance. They have been betrayed.

And yet hope remains.

I sense a change surging through the magic of

*this world. A great rebalance is coming. A path
lies ahead where the life forces of the old-Kind
will endure to spawn more of their kind.*

*I pray to the Creator that this will happen
soon.*

Extract from the final page of the
Chronicles of Havanthya

1

THE REMAINS

*T*he death-song still thrummed through Jonas's veins.

Blood dripped from the colossal blade he held. This iron scimitar had once belonged to the Gaoler himself, but Grashkor would never hold it again. The Kind's body lay at Jonas's feet. His mottled green hide bulged under thick armour plates as the stump of his neck leaked gore. His head had rolled a few paces away and lay face-down on the blood-stained ground, still wearing his horned helmet.

As the blaze of the death-song slowly ebbed from his own blood, Jonas became aware of his surroundings: the light breeze tickling the feathergrass, the shattered remains of his tribe's huts, the sound of a girl's voice.

"You're hurt," she said.

Halima – once his prisoner, now his companion – stood at a safe distance. Her eyes darted between the sword in Jonas's hand and Grashkor's corpse, as if she were afraid to approach the brutal scene. Jonas couldn't blame her. The fight with the skin-Kind Gaoler had been short, shocking and brutal. Long ago, Halima would have been in danger too: the frenzy for killing that dwelled in Jonas's blood would have driven him to continue his spree. No one would have been safe. Not even someone he now called his friend. But the golden breastplate Jonas now wore helped quell the raging fire of his death-song.

"It's over," he told her. The danger, both of the battle and of his own unpredictable rage, had passed. "You're safe now."

Jonas tossed the ten-foot blade beside its former owner's corpse and went to retrieve his own weapons from where he'd dropped them. They were the curved Swords of What Was and What Will Be.

"Your arm's bleeding," Halima said as she crept forwards.

Jonas had forgotten about the wound – a deep gash to his forearm. He marvelled instead at the pale marks on his wrists, where until a few minutes ago the Gaoler's manacles had been fastened. For almost two years they had been a symbol of his bondage to the Pinnacles of the Damned, the prison Grashkor had ruled liked a vengeful tyrant. With just the power of his mind, the Gaoler had once been able to summon Jonas back to that terrible place. But no more. Grashkor's days were over, and in their brief duel the Gaoler himself had accidentally severed the enchanted metal of the manacles. In a single stroke, Jonas's thousand-year sentence had been scrubbed clean.

He was free.

"It's *my* wing you should be asking about," hissed Seth.

The ghost-Kind wyvern sat not far off, leaning against the felled hulk of the sacred sangwar tree where the shamans of Jonas's tribe had once worshipped. Its roots jutted into the sky. Seth cradled his injured wing as he inspected the wound Grashkor had given him.

"You'll heal," said Jonas. Already his own blood had clotted. Thanks to his connection to the ghost-Kind, it would be half a day at most until the skin had knitted back together. Within three days even the scarring would have vanished.

The wyvern scowled back, his slitted eyes narrowing.

Seth had saved Jonas's life many times. Without him, and the death-song channelled from the darkness of the Netherplane, Jonas would be but a fraction of the fearsome warrior he was. He was sure he would have perished long ago.

The two of them were bonded, their life force shared. When Seth had received the blow from Grashkor's sword, the same cut had appeared on Jonas's arm. Should one die, the other would perish too. Closer than brothers, their very spirits were one.

But much like brothers, they weren't always friends.

The shamans of Jonas's tribe had viewed Seth as a gift from the gods, sent to aid them in fighting off the encroaching insect-Kind. And Seth's fearsome companionship had indeed been a blessing in times of mortal need. But others viewed the wyvern as a terrible curse. Humans and new-Kind alike feared Jonas because of his connection with Seth. They called him "Slayer".

"You saved my life," said Halima. "Thank you."

"And you saved mine," said Jonas, sheathing the twin swords across his shoulders. The small human girl had pushed him out of the way a fraction before Grashkor would have crushed them both.

"Spare me the back-slapping," said Seth. "We shouldn't have come here in the first place. We should have taken this human rebel directly to Grashkor. Then none of this would have happened and my wing would still be properly attached to my body."

"We didn't choose to come here, remember?" said Jonas. "It was Gael's magic."

Yet it couldn't be by chance alone that the crow-Kind wizard Gael had teleported them to this exact spot. *Home*. Or what remained of it.

Once a thriving settlement of tents and cooking fires, now the site of three bloody fights.

The first had happened when Jonas was thirteen, when his family and tribe had been massacred by an unknown force. Jonas himself, the sole survivor, had been blamed, imprisoned in the Pinnacles of the Damned. He was certain – *almost* certain – that he wasn't responsible, but until he learned the truth of that fateful day, he couldn't rest.

The second battle had been only a few days ago, when he and Seth had slaughtered a small army of insect-Kind, whose corpses still littered the ground among the wreckage of the huts. Among these also lay the remains of Rahziin, the cat-Kind sorcerer Jonas had spared from prison.

The just-concluded duel with Grashkor made it three fights. The Gaoler had tracked them here, determined to kill Jonas for disobeying his orders. And he would have succeeded if it weren't for the golden breastplate gleaming across Jonas's chest. It alone had given him the strength and focus to fight back.

But the breastplate was more than mere armour, Jonas knew. It was a symbol of what could be. He'd received it from the ghostly spirit of Thom, the long-dead Master of the Kind, in the catacombs beneath Skin-Grave. Thom had told Jonas that he was to take up the role of Master.

The *Last* Master, who could unite humans and Kind once more and for ever.

Jonas didn't see how he could do such a thing. He was no hero, that much was certain. He was a killer. Death-touched, blood-stained, with the screams of the dying forever ringing in his ears. Humans didn't trust him, especially not the rebels who wanted to overthrow the Kind. And they had good reason not to. He'd led the Emperor's forces right to their camp in the forests outside Skin-Grave, and many of them had been slaughtered. More specifically, Seth was the one who'd revealed the location of their camp, but to the humans that distinction made no difference. And why should it? Seth was Jonas, and Jonas was Seth – they were two sides of the same coin.

Jonas turned to the ghost-wyvern now. His green scales shimmered in the sun as he fussed at his wing. When they were young, they'd been inseparable. Trusted confidants who'd shared everything. But that had changed. Now Seth often disappeared for hours or days at a time, though this suited Jonas fine. He needed space – they both did. On more than one occasion, Jonas had told Seth to leave him for good, but the wyvern always eventually returned. Seth had always claimed to be trying to protect Jonas, but how true was that, really? Jonas knew Seth wasn't always honest with him. If their interests diverged, Jonas knew all too well whose agenda Seth would follow.

A gasp from Halima shook Jonas from his thoughts. He moved to her side to see what had startled her.

Something was happening to Grashkor's body. It seemed to be collapsing in on itself: desiccating before their eyes, the flesh turning to dust as it fell from the bones. The thick armour plates hit the ground with dull clangs. Soon, all that remained of the Gaoler's body was a skeleton with a tumorous black organ at its centre. To Jonas's astonishment, it still pumped softly under his bulging ribcage.

"What is that thing?" whispered Halima.

"*That*," said Seth, walking closer and peering with curiosity at the pulsating object, "is the heart of Equinias."

"Who?" said the human girl.

Seth gave her a smug look. "Equinias was a ghost old-Kind, said to feed on the souls of his enemies. Thom defeated him with some help from his companion Helenya – so they say. Grashkor must have stolen it from somewhere."

"But how did it get *inside* him?" asked Jonas.

Then Grashkor's skeleton crumbled too. The monstrous heart twitched and bulged as if something within was trying to escape. Shreds of black smoke flowed from it, quickly taking the shape of wraith-like humans and Kind. Their faces were contorted in anguish, their limbs desperately reaching out as they escaped. With them came deathly whispers, similar to those Jonas had heard in the catacombs under Skin-Grave. Jonas felt the death-song rise within him, but the golden breastplate kept his murderous urges in check.

"What are they?" whispered Halima.

Jonas was about to say he thought he recognised one of the figures – an ox-Kind named Bovirix he'd once dragged to the Pinnacles at Grashkor's behest – but the wraiths answered as one, their voices wrapping around one another in a hissing chorus:

"*We are those who died in Grashkor's custody, those he consumed to prolong his wretched life. Now that we are free, we will have our revenge! Revenge on the Slayer who took us to our tormentor!*"

The ghostly spectres whipped through the air towards Jonas, extending claws and baring their teeth. Jonas flailed his arms as he felt scratches tear across his face. Shadowy claws sought his neck and his legs were seized. Black wisps of evil found his ears and nostrils, forcing themselves inside. Whatever these shades of the dead were, he couldn't fight them. Even if he could, there were far too many. He felt them pull at his eyelids as he was lifted off the ground. They were trying to carry him away.

"Help me!" he cried. "Seth! Do something!"

Suddenly the spirits were gone, evaporating to nothing. Jonas hit the ground hard. Winded, he looked up to see the black clouds dispersing like smoky soot blown from a cold campfire. Seth hadn't moved, but Halima was standing beside the black heart, her dagger buried up to the hilt in Equinias's soul-prison. The foul organ was finally completely still.

"They certainly didn't like you much," said Seth. He was grinning.

"Glad you think it's funny," said Jonas. He glanced about nervously. "Are they gone for good?"

"To the Land of What Was, where the dead belong," replied Seth. "Even old-Kind aren't immortal, and Grashkor was using their life force as well as the heart of Equinias to live unnaturally long."

He flapped his wings once, experimentally, and hissed. Jonas felt the sting too: a twang of pain sang through his body in sympathy.

"Why didn't you ever mention this before?" he asked.

"Was it important?" challenged Seth.

That's not the point, thought Jonas. Once again, Seth was keeping things from him. How many more secrets did the wyvern have?

"So they're spirits of the dead, like the ghost of Thom, the Last Master?" said Halima. "Is he in the Land of What Was as well?"

Seth rolled his eyes. "The living have such a limited understanding of ghosts," he said. "Ghost is an element in and of itself. The only element that isn't physical matter. Ghost-Kind can be many things and they can be tethered to the living world for many reasons. In some cases, by unnatural dark magic, as you have just seen. Or they might be connected to a particular person simply to haunt them for their crimes." He looked down his scaled nose at Halima. "It's hard for a human mind to fathom."

She hiked her chin. "And what is the case with you, ghost-wyvern? Why do you stick around?"

Jonas caught a flinch of distaste in Seth's features. "Some of us are yoked by destiny," he said. As he turned away, his solid physical form shimmered to a translucent green ghost that only Jonas could see.

Halima huffed, as though only partially satisfied by the cryptic answer, then turned north. "We should get going," she said. "We need to reach the rebel stronghold in Anoros."

"You don't need to follow this little human girl," muttered Seth. When he was in ghost-form, only Jonas could hear his voice. "You can still change your mind, and you should. Your destiny lies elsewhere."

Jonas didn't reply. He didn't want to give the wyvern the satisfaction of an argument and he knew full well that Seth disapproved of his new human friend. Besides, he'd already made his decision. For so long, he'd been driven by his desire to escape the

Pinnacles at any cost, hunting down fugitives for the Gaoler.

Not any more. Now he was free and his choices were his own to make.

Halima was cleaning her dagger of gore from Equinias's heart. She glanced over at Jonas and smiled shyly. Perhaps she was still a little afraid of him, even now. But when she looked at him, Jonas thought she saw something else too: hope for what he could be, if Thom's prophecy proved true. A saviour, a healer, a deliverer from the terrible oppression humans suffered under the new-Kind.

Not for the first time, Jonas thought to himself how much she resembled his cousin Fran, in mannerisms as well as her delicate looks. At first, Halima had just been another bounty for Jonas: a thief working for the human rebels, sent to steal the powerful Tablets of the Creator from beneath Skin-Grave.

At the time, Jonas had cared little for the war between Kind and the human rebels who fought against their oppression – all he'd wanted was to reduce his sentence and continue his quest to find out who'd actually killed his tribe.

But those straightforward times were behind him. Jonas had fallen in with the human rebels and their witch mentor, the Reader. She had called for a war unlike any other, when the new-Kind would wield dangerous ancient magic drawn from the Tablets of the Creator. This was pure magic from the Netherplane. If she was right, Jonas was the only one who could stand against the annihilation of all humans.

He knew as well as anyone that there were those in power in the capital of Whitestone who'd happily see the extinction of humanity – people like the Arch Protector Malachai, the zealot leader of the murderous Order of the True.

And when Thom had given him the breastplate beneath Skin-Grave, he'd shown Jonas another path. One not guided by vengeance and the lure of the death-song, but something better. The promise of a different future, when the mysterious *Cleansing* would bring about a great rebalancing. The humans hoped this would mean an age of peace, and called it *New* Havanthya, named after the golden age when Thom had lived – a kingdom in which old-Kind and humans had lived in harmony.

Everyone seemed to have a slightly different idea about Jonas's destiny, including Seth, of course.

Gael had told Jonas that he'd have to choose among them.

The old-Kind had come to their rescue in the catacombs under Skin-Grave in the form of a giant white crow. If it weren't for him, they'd surely have been imprisoned and tortured by Malachai. Jonas would have liked to talk to Gael again, but the ancient crow-Kind had vanished as quickly as he'd appeared.

Jonas had never had allies before. This was partly because he'd never known who to trust, but also because of the terrible peril he knew faced anyone who might stand beside him. The death-song always waited within him. Before he'd been given the golden breastplate, berserker violence could seize him at any moment. Caught in its song, he'd kill friend and enemy alike.

He stared northwards. A long journey was what he needed to clear his thoughts. It would be dangerous crossing the mountains where new-Kind roamed, but he had faith in the blades across his back. Seth might not approve of their new mission, but he was an invaluable travelling companion, alert to threats that Jonas couldn't see.

A movement behind one of the torn tents snagged his gaze.

"Fran?"

The name escaped his lips, because she was

standing right there, not thirty paces away, wearing her sable fur hat. His cousin. Though he understood it couldn't be – Fran was dead, along with all his family – his feet still carried him in that direction. By the time he reached the spot, she was gone. Peering into the tent, though, he saw the hat lying on the ground, half buried in dirt blackened by dried blood. The very spot where she must have died.

Halima came jogging after him. "What's up?"

"I saw my cousin," he said quietly.

Halima frowned, then put a hand on his arm. "You've had a hard day."

Jonas tore his eyes from the hat and allowed her to usher him away.

Seth stood not far away, watching him carefully. The wyvern looked uncharacteristically troubled.

"You saw her too, didn't you?" said Jonas.

Instead of replying, Seth flapped his wings and soared away in a stiff, unsteady flight.

Jonas recalled the wyvern's words about ghosts and about haunting. If Fran was real, if his mind *wasn't* playing tricks, perhaps his dead cousin was trying to tell him something. Maybe it was about what really happened here, in his village – about what really killed his tribe. But then why had she run away?

Maybe all ghosts were as unpredictable as Seth . . .

Halima began to pick through a neighbouring tent, but Jonas lingered. Not for the first time he felt paralysed, tethered by the mysteries of the past but pulled to the uncertainties of the future.

Trapped between the worlds of What Was and What Will Be.

2

INTRIGUES AT COURT

From above, the Netherplane looked like a vast, storm-shaken sea of black shadow.

Lana was dreaming, suspended in the air above the volatile sea, watching its surface pitch.

Waves of shadow unfurled into the shapes of cities past and future, of mountain ranges and even of half-formed creatures she knew from myths. These were elemental monsters made of fire or water or black stone, the oldest of the Kind who had once roamed the world.

These shadows were wrought of pure magic. The same pure power that engulfed the right side of Lana's own body. This shadow clung to her, showing everyone that she too was touched by magic.

Below her, unnatural-looking whirlpools formed. Shaped like ovals, the swirling currents made her head spin. The symbols of pure magic. These eddies manifested into the features of a face, half-concealed by a dark hood. As its lips moved, a voice shook the sky and echoed deep within Lana's skull.

"Come . . . deeper," it boomed.

Lana somehow knew who it was: the Creator. He who had first shaped the chaos into shadow and other elements. He who had brought into existence the Many Worlds. He had spawned the old-Kind and, when they were brought to the brink of extinction by humans, created the new-Kind with the last of their life force.

"*Deeper*," he said again.

Lana was afraid, but she was caught by the Creator's will, as was the Netherplane itself.

The shadows of the Netherplane's endless ocean tore apart and flowed together again to form a new vision. A desert landscape where humans were in locked in battle against the old-Kind, whom they fought with spears and swords. Lana knew the stories from her childhood, read by her mother – scenes from the famous *Chronicles of Havanthya*. This was the past – the Land of What Was.

The scene was washed away, and in its place

appeared a vast army of humans in modern dress, carrying scythes and clubs and woodcutters' axes. These were the rebels sought by her master, Arch Protector Malachai, leader of the Order of the True. The human rebels walked through a beautiful city of soaring spires, delicate arches and gleaming domes. A crow-Kind in a robe strode alongside a human woman.

Is this happening now? Lana wondered.

The army of humans and the city vanished, replaced by a boy in a golden breastplate. Lana recognised him as Slayer, the death-blessed young man she'd met under Skin-Grave. With him was a slight human girl – the rebel thief he'd rescued. Lana was now sure she was watching the present – the Land of What Is.

And finally, the roiling shadows of the Netherplane showed her a battle in that same spired city. The human rebels were in combat against Kind of every sort. There was a cacophony of clashing weapons and bloodcurdling cries. Caught in the grip of the Creator's will, Lana soared over the melee until she saw a figure standing apart. She gasped because it was *her*. Her hands were outstretched towards what looked like a giant eye – a portal. A rip in reality itself. And from it flowed a torrent of shadow magic, breaking around her body like a stone in a stream. The shadow's dark tendrils licked greedily over the battling troops and city buildings, turning all the humans it touched to ash. Lana wanted to look away, but couldn't. This was the great Cleansing that Malachai wanted. Was this the future?

If so, it meant nothing less than the destruction of all humanity.

"Why are you showing me this?" she cried.

The sea of shadow once more formed into the face of the Creator.

"The Land of What Will Be is yet unmapped, Lana Shadowscale."

"How can I stop it happening?" she asked.

"You cannot," said the Creator. "Not alone. Not until you—"

"—Wake up." A female voice cut through the borders of the dream.

The Creator's face lost its edges and sank back into the shadows.

"Until I *what*?" She begged the Creator to finish his sentence.

"Open your eyes, Lana."

Light rushed in, so bright that for a moment, Lana couldn't see. Then she saw Jun standing over her. "You were talking in your sleep again."

Lana sat up on her bed and looked around her chamber. Jun was her oldest friend, a human worker from Lana's family mines. Malachai had imprisoned her when they first arrived at Whitestone, but Lana had used her growing influence to free her friend. In public, Jun pretended to be a simple servant, but she was much more. Jun listened for news of what humans in the city were up to, and there was no one Lana trusted more for advice.

"I was dreaming . . . I think," said Lana. Yet she knew it had been more than a dream.

"So it seemed," said Jun. "The Creator, again?"

Lana swung her legs from the bed and nodded dumbly. The shadow covering the right side of her body shifted to form the shapes of magical runes, as if still troubled by the visions. Fear tickled her heart. Was this what her mother had felt? A power steadily growing inside her that was enticing and impossible to resist?

Until it drove her mad.

Lana had been having these episodes ever since she'd set eyes on the Tablets of the Creator. Those colossal stone monuments, covered in ancient spells, had been destroyed in the collapse of the caverns under Skin-Grave, but both Malachai and the human rebels had taken transcriptions. Their arcane sorcery was not lost. If they were able to translate the runes, they'd be able to channel raw magic directly from the Netherplane.

Was it raw magic that I saw sweeping over the battle?

"What happened this time?" asked Jun, gripping the edges of the heavy embroidered drapes. A shaft of sunlight cut across the marble floor like a blade.

Lana looked at her friend's concerned expression. Humans were her allies, yet the vision had placed her at the very centre of their massacre. *Why would I ever do such a thing?*

"It was hard to make sense of," Lana said, which was true enough.

Jun seemed satisfied with the answer. "Well, you need to get up anyway. You won't get votes lying in bed." She flung open the door to a wardrobe and took out Lana's robes of the Order of the True. "I'll bring water for washing."

After Jun left the room, Lana walked to the curtains, pulled them back fully, then stepped out on to the balcony. Servants, messengers and delivery boys crisscrossed the square below, as well as lizard-Kind soldiers who wore the red robes of the Emperor's Own, his personal bodyguards. Arch Protector Malachai himself had given Lana this house, in recognition of her talents. Over the roofs of the grand administrative buildings and aristocratic residences, the Marble Palace itself soared. The morning sun picked out the sparkling facets of its walls. Like much of the city's architecture, it was constructed of the very marble Lana's family had once mined in the Burrows. This was the home of the Emperor himself, a bloated lizard-Kind nearing the end of his days.

But soon that would change. Soon, the throne could be *hers*.

The Emperor was abdicating, and several candidates were jostling for his seat of power, including Lana herself. Though the Shadowscale family had fallen from favour after her mother's madness, their star was rising again. They'd once been the foremost line in the kingdom. Indeed, Lana's ancestor, Elrith the Living Shadow, had been crowned the first new-Kind empress after crushing the human armies to end the Hundred Years' War. If Lana was clever, she too could achieve such power.

Her success would rely on sweet-talking courtiers with flattery and promises. She meant to begin with the Emperor himself, who would cast a vote for his successor. As part of her mission to impress him, she intended to complete her work on the new statues in the main square before the palace. Lana's shadow-magic gave her the ability to sculpt stone and other natural matter with the power of her mind. In the Burrows, she had been just a blunt tool, peeling granite from cavern walls, but here in Whitestone she could put her skills to more artistic uses.

Jun returned with a trolley holding a ewer of steaming water, towels and a wide basin.

"Is there any news that I should know?" asked Lana.

Jun closed the doors behind her. Spies were everywhere in Whitestone. Lana knew this as well as anyone. She used them herself to keep an eye on her rivals for the imperial throne. Jun was well connected to a network of human servants.

"Silash is gaining followers," she said. "Especially among the new-Kind lords and landowners."

Lana grunted. "I bet he is." Silash was a cunning and conniving gecko-Kind, and one of Malachai's closest allies. Her uncle, Bart, had told her that Silash disliked the Shadowscale dynasty, because in his youth he'd been rejected in love by Lana's mother. When Lana's mother's madness had set in, he'd been a key voice in ousting Lana's family from their home in Whitestone.

"There's also talk of a peace treaty with the rebels."

"Really? Who?" Whitestone was normally a hotbed of anti-human sentiment, so it was a surprise to hear of anything other than outright hatred of any human resistance movement.

"Some of the younger new-Kind courtiers and officials," said Jun. "They think we could even grant the humans a kingdom of their own in the north."

"I can't see that happening," said Lana as she began to bathe her scales.

"It *could* happen, though," said Jun. "If you were to press for the courtiers' support, they might give you enough votes to push through an alliance." Her eyes were earnest. "By imperial decree, the persecution of my people would end overnight."

Lana looked away, still haunted by her vision of mass death. She simply couldn't share it with Jun – not until she understood it herself.

"Do you even care?" asked Jun, her face suddenly hurt and hostile.

"Of course I do," said Lana.

Jun came closer, lowering her voice. "When people realise the extent of Malachai's injuries, they'll install someone of the same disposition. Someone cruel. Someone like Silash. We can't let that happen.

Some courtiers are already asking questions about where the Order of the True is keeping him."

Lana nodded and put her finger to her lips. There was a chance someone else was listening, even now, and she couldn't afford to be seen as anything but loyal to the Arch Protector. After being crushed under Skin-Grave, Malachai remained in the infirmary in the deepest recesses of the Temple of the Creator, being treated by wizards and doctors.

"Is there really no hope he'll get better?" asked Lana.

"He shows no sign of consciousness at all," said Jun.

"Long may that be," muttered Lana under her breath.

Dressed in the flowing robes of the Order of the True, Lana headed downstairs to the dining room where the table was laid for breakfast. Her little sister, Shahn, was there, as was her uncle, Bart, his plate piled high with dried cockroaches. A dozen or so other loosely connected family members were also present: sweet, simple Bart seemed to find new ones every day. The Shadowscales had been pariahs until a month ago, but now all sorts of cousins and hangers-on had crawled from the woodwork to bask in the glow of the family's new renown.

Shahn shoved back her chair and leapt up to give Lana a hug. "I've not seen you for days!" she said glumly. "You said we could tour the tropical gardens together."

"I've been working—" began Lana.

"You're *always* working," retorted her sister.

Lana held her at arm's length and smiled. "I'm apprentice to the Arch Protector," she said patiently. "The Emperor has had me sculpting all week. It's important I keep him happy." Shahn harrumphed. "There'll be plenty of time later for gardens and games," Lana added.

"Speaking of time," said Bart, "I could do with a few moments of yours before you scurry off." He belched loudly. "Small matters pertaining to the new estates we've been granted on the coast . . ."

"That can wait too," said Lana.

"There's the matter of the Burrows, as well. Productivity has fallen since we left."

"Then perhaps you could return for a few days and lend some encouragement," said Lana.

Bart's lips turned downward. Clearly he didn't relish leaving the luxuries of Whitestone any time soon. "Well, I suppose you're right . . ."

Lana smiled. "Of course, you must finish your breakfast first. It's a long journey. Now, I'm afraid I have business elsewhere."

Shahn had wanted to come to the main square too, but Lana dissuaded her. "It'll be dangerous," she said.

"But I'll be with you," said her sister.

"Exactly. I have enemies now. They may try to hurt me by harming you."

Shahn had accepted this, though Lana still felt bad as she entered the bustling streets with Jun at her side. On the balconies and stepped sides of the buildings, lizard-Kind were already basking in the morning heat.

"You were right to make her stay behind," said Jun, who must have sensed Lana's disquiet. "It would only take one assassin with a dagger."

"Have you heard of such threats?" asked Lana, a little alarmed.

"Not precisely," said Jun. "But in the minds of the humans, you're an ally of Arch Protector Malachai. And to everyone else, you're a rival for the Emperor's throne. That makes you, and those close to you, targets."

"Do I have *any* friends at all?" asked Lana.

"You have me," said Jun with a wink.

Not for the first time, Lana considered sending both Bart *and* Shahn back to the Burrows until after the election. Her uncle was largely a harmless nuisance, but Shahn was her responsibility. Lana would never forgive herself if any ill befell her.

A buzzing beetle droned overhead, startling her and making her shadows sway. "I swear that thing's been following me," she said, swatting at it.

"You're paranoid," said Jun as the insect flew off.

Lana felt much safer once they reached the main square, as the Emperor's Own paraded at regular intervals in front of the Marble Palace. Along one side of the square were statues of emperors and empresses past, culminating in the sculpture Lana had personally carved of the current ruler. She'd used considerable licence to reduce his belly and straighten his hunched back. in real life, she doubted very much that he'd be able to wield the axe depicted by the statue. These days the gluttonous ruler could barely stand from his cushioned basking couch.

At the start of the line of statues, there was a large awning with guards stationed at the entrance. Lana and Jun were waved inside with respectful nods from the scaled heads of the halberd-wielding guards. Inside, it was pleasantly warm, and rising before them was Lana's latest creation, a likeness of her ancestor Elrith the Living Shadow. The height of a two-storey building, it was almost complete, but the face itself was still a formless lump of stone.

Lana got to work straight away, throwing off her outer robe and releasing her shadow. Jun looked on, her lips parted in awe. Perhaps fear, as well. Lana lifted her arms and felt the surge of her powers. With just a sway of her fingers, she began to mould the marble like softened wax. Since being exposed to the Tablets of the Creator, her power felt limitless. As if it was growing inside her, with a desire of its own to reach out. It was sometimes quite . . . intoxicating.

Had her mother had felt this, too? Before she lost her mind?

Lahara had also been plagued by visions. She'd screeched mad prophecies until the day she took her own life. Lana had only been a little girl then, younger than Shahn was now. She focused on the marble to quell her disturbed thoughts.

Of course, no one knew exactly what Elrith had looked like; she'd ruled centuries ago. There were descriptions in some of the texts, but it was all vague, poetic stuff about "fierce beauty" and "piercing eyes". So Lana had based the appearance on that of her mother, or what she remembered of her in happier times. When it was finished, the statue would be a powerful statement that the Shadowscales were not ashamed of their past. They had been here from the beginning. They *belonged* at the seat of power.

And under Lana Shadowscale they were here to stay.

3

SONG OF THE SANGWAR TREE

*H*alima had been scavenging whatever she could from the camp. She'd asked Jonas if he minded, perhaps expecting some sentimentality about his lost tribe's possessions.

"They won't care," he told her. "They're dead, aren't they?"

And so she went from tent to tent, emerging with anything she found useful – iron tools, binding twine, a pair of fur gloves. Jonas sat on a rock, running a sharpening stone along his blades, watching the sparks die in the dusky light.

They *were* dead, all of them. But dead wasn't the same as gone. He was sure his cousin Fran's spirit lingered, but why? Did she blame him for what happened here? Or did she want him to find the truth and take vengeance for their deaths? If so, she might at least have given him a hint.

Jonas tried to recall her features when he'd glimpsed her ghost. Though she'd been thirty paces away, he couldn't help but think she'd seemed scared. But of what?

Not me, surely . . .

Jonas shook his head. He couldn't let the past hold on to him. Not if he was to fulfil Thom's prophecy.

Halima approached with a leather slingshot hooked over one shoulder and a flint-case in hand. Jonas smiled to himself. He and his friend Saul had played at target practice on the bluff above the settlement, aiming at crows. Saul hadn't been a fighting sort at all, preferring to play jaunty tunes on his flute. Jonas hoped that his friend had died quickly and painlessly on that fateful day.

He looked across to the tent that had once been Saul's home, willing *his* ghost to appear. The tent flaps stirred in a gentle breeze, but there was no sign of his friend. Jonas would have liked to see him, though he had to wonder what expression Saul's ghost would have carried. Perhaps Jonas didn't need any more haunting looks full of recrimination.

Halima stuffed her latest finds into her pack.

"Shall we get going?"

Jonas sheathed his swords. "Let's wait for dark," he said. "We're both fugitives now – the Arch Protector will have a bounty on our heads, and every Kind in the kingdom will want to claim it."

"He's surely dead," said Halima. "Half the catacombs collapsed on him, didn't they?"

"Maybe so," said Jonas. "But that just means there'll be a new Arch Protector, and he or she will be just as bad."

Halima didn't protest. She trusted his judgement, Jonas thought. At the very least, she knew she needed him at her side to stay alive.

"Where's the ghost-wyvern?" she asked.

Jonas shrugged, staring at the sky. "Close, probably. Who knows. He'll find us if he wants to."

"You don't sound very fond of him," said Halima.

"It's . . . complicated," said Jonas. He stood from his rock. "There's something I need to do before we leave."

He walked to the shaman's tent. One side of it was torn open and the other was stained with an arc of dried blood. Inside, among various sacred apparatus and instruments, he found an incense dish and burner, both made of hammered copper. Jonas had never been one for rituals; he'd always found them boring. But this might be the last chance he had to say goodbye properly to his people. Their bodies had been left to rot on the ground where they fell, so perhaps their spirits were barred from the Land of What Was because they'd never had a proper burial. If so, he could now put that right.

He carried the incense over to the sangwar stump and placed it on the ground. He dropped to his knees beside it.

"What's that thing?" whispered Halima.

"Sangwar trees have long been sacred to my people," replied Jonas. "We once lived alongside them on the rich shores of Nara Lake, but insect-Kind invaded those lands. Before my tribe fled, they felled then uprooted this tree to take with them. They would circle their tents around it whenever they moved camp. It was said to offer protection." He snorted. "So much for that, huh?"

Halima gave a thin, sympathetic smile. Jonas guessed that she too had seen plenty of her friends and family perish.

Neither of us are strangers to death.

This sacred sangwar had been felled by his great-grandmother, the Chief of Chiefs, a great warrior who'd united the tribes to fight off insect-Kind . . . for a time, anyway. Jonas's father had said Jonas would become the new Chief of Chiefs, and that he would drive off the insect-Kind barbarians to the south and the new-Kind lords to the north.

For so long this had seemed like an impossible fantasy. But so much had changed.

If Thom was to be believed, the golden breastplate might allow its wearer to unite not just the tribes of Morta and the plains, but all humans and Kind across the Four Kingdoms.

Was such a thing truly possible?

Jonas scooped the red dust from the base of the stump and rubbed it between his hands and across his cheeks and forehead. All the while, he gazed at the images carved on to the stump – the Earth Father and Sky Mother chasing each other in a perpetual dance, meeting only to the east and west, at the hours of sunrise and sunset. Other carvings told the story of What Was, What Is and What Will Be, each strand twisted around the other, as history, present and future run in parallel — or so the shamans would say. Jonas never paid much attention to the shamans, but he found now that he remembered their words. They were carved inside him, like the rings of a tree. He lit the incense oil and let his lips sound the ancient chants.

As the sweet smoke looped around his head and

found his nostrils, he felt his head swim. The haze of smoke blurred the outline of Halima and the tents around him. Above his own voice, he heard the songs of others, insistent and getting louder. Then he saw them, seated at his side – the shamans, their faces also daubed with red dust. And beyond them, the rest of the tribe, young and old. His cousins and uncles. They all sang the same words. The words that were also on Jonas's own lips.

Then they suddenly fell silent.

They clutched each other with looks of pure terror. Some scrambled away. Jonas turned to see what had frightened them. A few metres above the sangwar, the sky had split open like a gash. It revealed a pure blackness beyond. Though night hadn't yet fallen, this was a patch of midnight. Whispers trickled from the wound in the air. They were deathly with menace and seething with hatred. Suddenly, something horrific was among them.

It was a sinuous, flying Kind. Red flames licked its winged body and clawed legs, making its true outline hard to discern. Heat seared Jonas's face as the creature descended on his people, turning their bodies to ash and silencing their screams. It swept back and forth over the fleeing tribesfolk with its searing claws, sparing no one in its massacre. One by one they fell, burned to the ground or sliced to pieces. The powerful Kind was greedy for death and merciless in its slaughter. It only stopped when everyone was dead.

Almost everyone . . .

A stifled wail from one of the tents made Jonas and the beast turn as one towards the sound. There she was – his cousin, Fran. She was hiding behind a tent, just as her ghost had been. This time, there was no doubting the expression in her young face. Grief at the scene of death. Horror before the carnage. Terror as a monster turned to her.

"Jonas?" she cried.

"Run!" he yelled.

The Kind moved first, its flame-licked body burning towards her. Jonas broke into a sprint a fraction of a moment later. He could save her if he could reach her first.

He somehow kept pace with the flying creature. Together, they closed in on his cousin as she remained transfixed, eyes wide with fear.

"Jonas! Stop!"

Fran's lips had moved, but the voice wasn't hers. It came from elsewhere. But the Kind was almost on her and Jonas knew he couldn't make it in time. The creature's jaws opened and the heat of its flames tore through the dusty air. Jonas drew one of his swords, lifting it to strike . . .

"Jonas, no! Please!"

Suddenly, the heat was gone. The creature and Fran too. At his feet, Halima was crumpled. Her arms shielded her face as he towered over her with the Sword of What Was raised above his head.

Halima sensed him hesitate and scurried away on her backside, her eyes locked on him.

Slowly, Jonas lowered the blade, turning a slow circle. Darkness had fallen. The camp was empty. It was again a lonely expanse of silent tents with the ghostly shape of the sangwar reaching for the sky with roots like twisted fingers.

"Are you . . . back?" whispered Halima.

He stared at the rebel girl. For a second, she was Fran again, but the moment quickly passed.

"I'm so sorry," he said, his voice a croak. "I *saw* her. I saw what happened."

"What do you mean?" she said.

"I was in the Land of What Was. I watched the creature that killed my people."

"A creature? An insect-Kind?"

Jonas shook his head. "An old-Kind, I think. It was made of fire." He closed his eyes to recall its shape. He remembered the words the cat-Kind

Rahziin had spoken to him before her death.

They fall before a tide of rippling air. A beast with six limbs and no sides. It stalks through your people, slashing a prophecy in blood. A creature of the past!

"She was telling the truth," he mumbled.

"Who?"

"Rahziin. She was my prisoner, before you – a cat-Kind priestess hunted by the Order of the True. I let her go."

Halima frowned. "You weren't a very good bounty hunter by the sounds of it."

Jonas ignored her. "She promised me to tell me what happened here," he said. "And in a way, she did."

"I think we should leave this place," said Halima, suddenly serious. "It's not good for you, or me."

Jonas nodded. The vision he'd just experienced was a memory that had been somehow locked away, either by trauma or because of shamanic magic. Did that mean there were others? Secrets in his own mind he had yet to uncover?

He tried to remember what else Rahziin had said, just before she was killed.

The shamans chant a music of death. It is the only way! They are destiny's sacrifice. The Mothers said I would glimpse the purpose of the Creator. It is the start of the Cleansing! One of three branches of fate designed in the Netherplane. But which sacrifice will bring terrible renewal?

What did it mean? That his tribe were meant to die, in order for some greater destiny to unfold? Thom had said the Cleansing might bring peace and balance, but what happened to his tribe was a brutal slaughter.

If that was fate, I want no part of it.

4

THE FOREST
OF FEAR

"*H*a! Go on, Slayer. That's it!"

Gael leaned forward in his seat as the carriage rocked over the rutted road. Felix, his beetle scribe, hovered in front of him, projecting images of the battle between Jonas and Grashkor, Gaoler of the Pinnacles. Or rather, the *former* Gaoler.

Jonas hefted the massive, curved blade, which was even longer than he was tall.

"Finish him!" roared Gael.

The Reader opened one eye, and looked across to the crow-Kind with disdain. "Can you keep the noise down, you old bird? Some of us are trying to sleep."

"Well, I'm sorry, but it's exciting!" said Gael. He

waved a hand, and the projection paused right at the moment Jonas's sword met the Gaoler's neck. Grashkor's eyes were wide with shock as though he'd just registered that his head was about to be disconnected from his body.

"It's the third time you've watched it," said the Reader. "Surely that dampens the suspense somewhat?"

"I told you he was special," said Gael. "Now that he has the golden breastplate, he can fulfil his destiny."

"Hmm," said the Reader doubtfully.

"Anyway, keep your voice down," said Gael. "You're supposed to be my servant, remember?"

"The driver is loyal to our cause," said the Reader. "Which is more than I can say for Slayer."

Gael sighed. "Thom's ghost chose him. What greater proof do you need that he's the new Master of the Kind?"

"I suppose it would be nice if he hadn't betrayed our encampment to the Emperor's legionaries," said the Reader. A fleeting expression of pain twitched through her features. "Many died. And many of them were my friends."

"That wasn't him," said the crow-Kind. "It was that ghost-wyvern of his."

"They are bonded," said the Reader. "One and the

same. And as long as the death-song burns through him, he's a danger to all."

"That's hardly his fault," said Gael.

"But you cannot deny it's a problem," the Reader replied.

Gael was silent. She had a point. Not that it changed his faith in the boy. Killing Grashkor was a declaration that he'd taken the side of the human rebels against the Emperor and all those Kind who'd happily wipe them from existence.

"You should really watch this bit though," he said, trying to lighten the mood. "I swear Grashkor's eyes are still blinking when his head rolls to a stop."

"I've had my fill of slaughter," said the Reader. "How many of those beetle spies have you got anyway?" She waved a dismissive hand at Felix.

Gael smiled. "I'm surprised you don't know," he said. "After all the spying *you've* done, Roshni."

"All for a good cause," she retorted.

Gael plucked the flying beetle from the air and stowed it in the folds of his cloak. He'd met the Reader when she'd been in the guise of a pitiable servant. He'd rescued her from punishment and made her his assistant. At the time, she'd told him her name was Roshni – which might still prove to be true – but this concealed the fact that she was actually the infamous magic-Kind known as the Reader: a powerful psychic and mentor to the human rebels. In her position as Gael's assistant, she'd manipulated him into giving her the talon of the old-Kind phoenix Aephos, and she'd convinced him to support the human cause.

Gael shuffled across the carriage's bench and tugged aside the curtain to peer outside. They were passing through a deserted village. Collapsing farm buildings sagged alongside weed-filled fields between broken-down fences. Among the ruins he spied the remains of a forge.

"This is Arndal!" he said. "Birthplace of Thom."

"Correct," the Reader said. "Not far now."

"I'm fairly sure I'd have heard if there was a rebel stronghold this close to Skin-Grave."

"Believe it or not, there *are* some things you don't know, Gatekeeper."

Gael ignored the jab and stared out at the sad remains of the village. "They say his first sword was a wooden one," he whispered.

"I know the stories," said the Reader. "But I'm not interested in legends of the past. It's the future that's important."

"Past, present and future are all one," Gael said.

"Oh good. Riddles," said the Reader.

Gael crossed his arms. "No matter how you understand time, I know Jonas *is* the future."

"He's *one* future," replied the Reader wearily. "Alia is another. She's wise and courageous and has the blood of the Masters in her veins."

"Yet it was Jonas who Thom chose," said Gael.

He knew the Reader favoured the human warrior, Alia, as leader of the rebellion. He'd given up trying to convince her otherwise. What would be, would be. Though that wasn't to say he didn't have his own favourite and would do what he could to push the scales in Jonas's favour.

The Reader leaned forward, and her tone became more earnest. "I sensed great conflict in his heart. His connection to death makes him unpredictable."

"He is part ghost. This gives him power," said Gael. "The future is his to make; his to bend to his will."

"Bend? Perhaps. But what if he's the one who *breaks*? What if his destiny crushes him? What if it turns him to evil?"

"Many think the element of ghost is sinister but in truth, it's neither good nor bad," said Gael. "It is nothing more or less than what is made of it. Much the case for just about anything, I'd say."

"Another lecture," said the Reader.

"Well, you are my apprentice," said Gael mockingly. "Speaking of which, if you wouldn't mind checking the instruments?"

She scowled, but opened the wooden case on the floor between them.

Within, cushioned by velvet, were Gael's tools. He had insisted Roshni retrieve them from his chambers in the Hallowed Vale before they set off: an anemograph, a barometograph and a percepticon, as well as vials of petrifactor and universal antidote. Plus some spare beetles, their wings curled around them in a way that resembled chrysalises. He took out the barometograph and tapped the side, watching the needle bob.

"Look here," he said. "You might learn something."

Despite being a bit disgruntled, the Reader was clearly intrigued.

"There's magical disturbance in the atmosphere," he said, examining the meter. "The elements are in conflict."

"And . . . ?"

"A great rebalancing is needed," said Gael.

The Reader leaned back and folded her arms. "Then perhaps you should focus on helping Alia. Every time she tries to speak with Aephos, the phoenix flies away. The old-Kind keeps to the slopes of the Stonewind Volcano."

"Old-Kind can be stubborn," said Gael. "Alia hasn't proven herself a Master of the Kind. There's no reason for Aephos to obey her."

"I've given her the talon that woke the phoenix," said the Reader. "It has great power over the old-Kind."

"Yes," conceded Gael. "The talon is a key, but it's not a collar. She can't expect to raise a creature like Aephos from slumber and pat it on the head like a dog."

He turned his attention back to the barometograph, partly to conceal his face and his thoughts from the Reader. He didn't know how deeply she could see into his mind or the secrets he was keeping regarding the red jewel in his possession. It allowed the holder to speak with the old-Kind, but he knew full well that Alia trying to tame Aephos would only infuriate the phoenix more. In any event, he had no intention of giving the jewel to anyone except Jonas.

There were scrolls in the Hallowed Vale that told of Thom riding on Aephos, bending her flight to his will. Gael had never seen such a thing. Indeed, he could scarcely imagine it possible.

But that didn't stop him hoping.

After they'd travelled for another hour or so, the cart lurched to a stop. A hatch opened between the driver's seat and their sheltered compartment. "Mistress," came a gruff voice. "I think you should look at this."

Gael gathered his robes about him, opened the carriage door and stepped down. They'd reached the edge of a tangled forest, and the track ahead narrowed as it entered the trees. From high branches hung sticks fashioned into the shape of humans. A gentle breeze ruffled Gael's feathered head.

"What are they?" he asked the Reader, who'd also jumped down from the carriage.

"Charms to ward off evil," she replied. "Made by the bear- and wolf-Kind clans who've forsaken this place." She nodded towards the treeline. "We should get out of sight in case there are Kind on the lookout."

"In there?" said the driver. He eyed the woods warily, clearly less than happy about the idea.

"Not you. You should return to the city," the Reader told him.

They gathered their belongings from the carriage, bade the driver farewell and set out side by side into the gloom between the trees. Gael kept his oscilloscope to hand, eyeing the blue vapour that swirled inside the glass cylinder. The air was cooler underneath the canopy, with a damp scent. They followed a path, if you could call such a scant trail a path. It was certainly nowhere near wide enough for a carriage. The forest floor was covered in layers of dried leaves which deadened the sound of their footsteps. Not a single bird or squirrel disturbed the branches above.

"They used to call this place the Forest of Fear," muttered the Reader. Her voice was flat.

"Very menacing," said Gael, rolling his eyes. Though if he were honest, he was a *little* afraid. What little sunlight filtered to the ground seemed drained of warmth. And though the forest seemed devoid of animal life, he felt quite sure that *something* lurked nearby. It made his feathers bristle. Sure enough the vapour in the oscilloscope was moving more erratically, changing colour to violet.

"There's some sort of portal nearby," he whispered. Odd that he didn't already know about it.

"Not exactly," said the Reader with a slight smile. She was obviously enjoying being in charge for a change.

Gael turned a dial to locate the correct frequency.

The gas changed colour to turquoise and settled into a wave pattern. "Interesting . . ."

"Go on," said the Reader.

"Spatial manipulation," said Gael. "A portal, but not to another world." He moved the oscilloscope from side to side and then up and down, watching the wave pattern change. "A pocket dimension," he muttered. "A world hidden *within* this one . . ." He closed the antennae on the instrument. "Pass me the rockglass lens from my case." He handed the oscilloscope back and rummaged in his cloak, pulling out his monocular. He unclipped the blue crystal lens.

"Which is the rockglass?" asked the Reader, poring over the case.

"The pink one," he said.

She fished it out and passed it over. He inserted it and brought the monocular to his eye. "I knew it!" he said as he saw between the trees a winding red path. "The Master's Road!"

"Correct," she said.

Gael had read of its existence in the *Chronicles of Havanthya*. In ancient times it was said that a Master had to prove himself or herself by walking the Road and exerting their will over four Kind on their journey. Many had perished trying.

"We'll reach our stronghold by following it," said the Reader.

Gael set off again with renewed vigour. His heart was thumping in excitement too. He had the sense that history must be repeating itself. Jonas had already defeated the Gaoler. Perhaps if he were to defeat three old-Kind he might find his way here? Once that happened, even the Reader couldn't deny his destiny.

With frequent checks through the rockglass lens, Gael led the way between the trees. Eventually they reached a strange, twisted archway looming among the trees. It was covered in moss, and at first he thought it was some sort of malformed tree itself, but on closer inspection it seemed to be made from a hardened sap. He ran his finger across the jagged surface.

"The slime of Skurich," said the Reader. "One of the old-Kind defeated by Thom." She glanced around anxiously.

"I'd have sensed if we were being followed," said Gael. "How much further is it?"

The Reader gestured to the arch. "We're here," she said.

Gael frowned. Through the arch he could see only more forest, dense and impenetrable.

"After you," he said.

The Reader obliged, stepping under the arch. As she did, she vanished.

Intriguing, thought Gael. He'd have to take more readings when he got a chance. With a deep breath, he followed the Reader across the threshold.

For a second, his feathers tingled from root to tip, and all was dark. But with another step, the light returned. He was again shoulder to shoulder with the Reader, but everything else had changed. The trees were gone and stretching before him was a grassland plain. Beyond that was a miracle: a towering city of gilded domes, soaring towers and delicate aqueducts. The great city was sheltered behind a thick stone wall, supported by buttresses and topped with battlements.

He'd seen illustrations of it in the *Chronicles*, brightly painted by the scholars of old. But it was even more astounding in person.

"Goodness me!" said Gael. "Is that . . ."

"It is indeed," said the Reader with a smile. "Welcome to the Lost City, Gatekeeper."

5

MOUNTAIN PERILS

The snow-topped peaks of the Quarg Mountains loomed ahead like watchful grey shadows.

Jonas led the way along the track through the foothills. He walked with care, both to keep noise to a minimum and to check for loose ground. A rockfall would bring attention, and that was the last thing they needed. Out here, one had to assume that everyone – Kind and human alike – was an enemy.

This was a perilous route and he'd rather not have come this way at all, but any trail closer to Whitestone was out of the question. Too many threats lurked near the city. Too many Kind and non-Kind who'd happily cut their throats for fame and a purse of silver.

He and Halima had been walking for hours in near-silence, and that suited Jonas fine. For her part, Halima didn't complain either. The quiet helped him focus on the path, his eyes peeled for prints of foot and paw. Distant campfires were easy to avoid, glowing orange against the darkness, or blowing their smoky tendrils downwind. But there'd be hunters in the mountains who knew better than to advertise their presence – bird scouts working on behalf of the Emperor, or other elite mercenaries seeking a payday by bringing back the head of Slayer.

No one knew how many human tribes occupied the mountain valleys, but the number was rumoured to be in the hundreds. These were said to be small bands, mobile if they needed to run, and ready to fight ferociously if they couldn't. One such party had discovered Jonas the day his own people were slaughtered. They'd found a lone, shocked boy, speechless and bloodstained amidst the carnage. It was easy to see how he'd gained a reputation for being cursed. He'd been speechless because he hadn't known how to answer their questions. He had no memory of what had happened. All he remembered was returning home from a solitary hunt to find everyone he'd ever known brutally slaughtered.

Now even he doubted that was the full truth. The vision he'd had back at the ruins of his tribe's camp suggested he'd been present at the massacre. Fran had shouted his name. If that meant he'd watched it happen, it was no wonder he'd blocked out the memory.

Visions . . . memories . . . The past and present and future . . . It's hard to know what's real at all.

He shook away his muddled thoughts. Dwelling on What Was might get them killed. He had to focus on their immediate surroundings. Jonas trusted himself to spot eagles or wolf-Kind, but insect-Kind were another matter. They could see far better than humans and could camouflage themselves especially well in a rocky landscape. Hopefully, Seth would warn them if there was danger ahead – he too had incredible night vision. Though Jonas couldn't sense his ghost-twin in the vicinity either. If Seth was near, then he'd also decided to keep himself well hidden.

Jonas wasn't surprised. Perhaps the wyvern wanted to avoid being questioned about *his* part in the massacre of the tribe. After all, if Jonas had been there, Seth surely was present too. He must have *seen* what happened. He must *know* who was responsible. Yet in the years since this had happened, he'd never mentioned it.

Thinking about it made Jonas's heart beat faster as anger stirred under his breastbone. Anger at Seth for his secrets, but also at himself for trusting the ghost-Kind so unquestioningly. For too long, he hadn't questioned Seth's purpose. He'd believed they were one, with the same interests and goals. But recent events had shown this to be a huge error.

What else had Jonas been wrong about?

For one thing, Seth had always claimed that their lives were dependent on one another – that if one perished, so would the other. But Jonas was no longer sure this was true. In port at the Ruby Isle, Jonas's death-song had brought him a vision of Seth's death at the hands of Orok the Crusher. This had been a sliver of What Will Be: the taste of a possible future. And in that brief, bloody glimpse, he'd seen that he himself did not die alongside Seth. Which meant one thing . . .

I can survive without him.

It was an intriguing, if terrifying, thought. The death-song came from Seth's connection to the Netherplane. Without Seth, there'd be no warnings of deaths to come. This second sight had helped

Jonas avoid countless mortal blows over the years. Without it, he'd be as vulnerable as any other human.

To abandon Seth for good – if that was even possible – might also mean never knowing what happened to his people.

"You should leave it behind," said Halima quietly.

Jonas turned to face her. Did she have psychic powers? Had she known what he was thinking?

"I'm sorry?" he said.

"The past cannot be altered," said Halima.

"I know I can't change it," said Jonas. "But I do need to understand it."

"The Reader can help you do that."

Jonas grunted. "So you keep saying."

"You know, the creature you described back at the camp sounds like a fire Elemental. I remember stories the rebels told, of old Havanthya, where evil wizards were able to open portals to the Netherplane and summon such Elementals. Maybe that's what your shamans did."

"Why would the shamans do that? They were killed."

"It might have been an accident," said Halima. "Or perhaps they were trying to summon the Elemental to help them fight your enemies. Such creatures are unpredictable."

It wasn't a very satisfactory explanation.

"You're angry," said Halima. "I can see you want someone to blame."

"Someone *is* to blame, and someone must pay."

"Why?" the girl asked. "The dead are ashes and dust. To be mourned."

"And forgotten?"

Halima shook her head. "Of course not. But vengeance will not help them. Or you."

Jonas bristled at the unsolicited advice. If it hadn't been for him, Halima would have been killed beneath Skin-Grave. But here she was, telling him what he needed.

"And you'd know all about this, would you?"

Halima smiled sadly. "For years I longed for revenge against the new-Kind who murdered *my* people. I dreamt of finding them and killing them. I fell asleep at night imagining their faces when I finally drove my blade between their ribs . . ." She trailed off, her eyes distant.

"So what happened?" asked Jonas.

"I met the Reader," said Halima. "She understood my pain and hate, but told me they would only get me killed. Sure, I might take one or two of my enemies with me, but when all was said and done, our blood would have been spilled for nothing and our names would be forgotten in the mists of What Was."

"All our names will be forgotten," said Jonas. "I'm not looking for fame."

Halima smiled. "I know that." She stared at him with an unnerving intensity. "But Thom seemed to think you'll have it anyway. You have a role to play, Jonas. A destiny. A purpose. The Reader can help you find that also."

"I suppose we'll see if—"

The death-song flooded his veins as his ears caught the snap of a twig in the foliage to their left. As time slowed, his first thought was to curse himself. He'd been busy debating with the girl instead of paying proper attention. He'd chosen a stupid route, with thick undergrowth that could easily conceal danger. He saw: *an arrow flying from the foliage, burying itself in Halima's neck. Himself rushing to her, and two more thumping into his thigh. Stumbling and falling. A final arrow piercing his heart.*

"Duck!" he shouted, reaching for her.

Halima obeyed, and the arrow whispered over her head, clattering off rocks nearby.

Jonas drew his swords and leapt into the bushes, letting the death-song guide his blade. It severed the bow, along with the man's hand, leaving the archer startled and staring at the spurting stump. Hearing a rustle at his back, Jonas crouched and leapt, performing a flip to land behind the second attacker. His blade longed for flesh, but Jonas somehow stopped himself. Instead, he turned the hilt in his hand and struck the man across the bridge of his nose with it. With a cry, the assailant crumpled.

Jonas marvelled at his self-control. Only days ago, he would have severed the man's head without a second thought, but something had stopped him. It must have been the golden breastplate, holding back the death-song's siren call.

A spiked club, coming from behind, caving in his skull . . .

Jonas spun away. The club missed, thumping into the ground, and he was faced with the man who wielded it – a giant with a bushy black beard. Jonas kicked his knees out from under him, and the brute crashed to the earth. The man was a sitting duck, begging to be hacked to pieces, but again Jonas managed to hold in check the murder in his heart. He looked between the trees in case there were any more attackers.

Then he heard Halima's scream.

He ran back to the path, leaving the attackers

injured and dazed. Fear mingled with the death-song. He'd failed to protect her. Another friend dead. Another corpse upon that towering pile.

Emerging once more on to the track, he saw that Halima was alive. But perhaps not for long. A man dressed in furs stood at her back, with what looked like a flint dagger held to her throat. The whites of Halima's panicked eyes were bright against the darkness.

"You're quick, Slayer," said the attacker, "but so is my blade. One more move, and she dies."

6

THE LIVING SHADOW

"**Y**ou should have a bodyguard," muttered Jun, who was standing a step behind Lana.

"No," she replied. "The people won't respect me if they think I'm afraid."

"You *should* be afraid," said Jun. "At least wear a veil in public. You attract too much attention."

From the stage, Lana looked upon the crowds amassed across the central square. It was true that most of the eyes were focused on her – or more specifically on the shadow that flickered down the right side of her face. There was plenty of curiosity in the stares of the spectators, but others also held barely concealed horror. But she met those glares defiantly. People needed to see that she wasn't cowed. That she was proud of her shadow-blessing.

"A leader can't live in fear," she said to Jun.

"You're not a leader yet," said her human friend. "You're just a girl, and one with many enemies. All the more reason to employ a couple of Kind with big swords."

"This discussion is over," said Lana briskly. "Remember your place, *servant*."

Jun growled under her breath, and Lana turned her attention back to the crowd, smiling in what she hoped was a reassuring way. On the other side of the stage, Bart and Shahn were both dressed in embroidered robes befitting the grand occasion. Lana was glad she'd summoned the old lizard back to Whitestone for this. Bart glowed with pride, waving to the crowd as though they were here to see *him*. Shahn looked a bit overwhelmed, but gave Lana a beaming smile when their gazes met.

Jun was right in some respects. Such a public occasion held many dangers, and Lana would rather her little sister wasn't here at all. Lana had told her as much, but Shahn had insisted. She was stubborn like that. Like their mother.

Maybe a bodyguard or two, placed subtly out of sight, would have been a good idea for Shahn's sake.

A horn trumpeted from the walls of the Marble

Palace. At its sound, the crowd fell silent. The palace's great gates opened, and the Emperor's retinue emerged. It took six servants, straining under the arms of a gilded palanquin, to carry the enormous komodo-Kind to the stage. The Emperor himself sat atop a cushioned platform, the folds of his reptilian flesh bulging around him like a loaf of bread taken too early from the oven and collapsing under its own weight.

Lana had seen him only a few days ago, but the ruler's decline was obvious. The old komodo-Kind looked sicker and frailer than ever, which made his abdication even more critical. It would be disastrous if he were to die without a successor named. This would be a recipe for in-fighting, or perhaps even civil war.

The Emperor surveyed the crowd through his narrowed, red-rimmed eyes as his tongue flicked between his thick lips. Rumour had it that Malachai had put some enchantment on him, to make him more vicious and paranoid than usual, all in service of the Arch Protector's campaign against humans. Could he have been poisoning the Emperor too, to hasten his illness?

Prodded by the imperial steward, the crowd greeted the ruler with cheers. The Emperor responded with a bob of his head that shook his jowls.

His bearers carried him – with considerable difficulty – up the steps towards the stage. When he spotted Lana, he beckoned for her to approach. Jun tried to follow, but Lana held up a hand so she'd remain at a distance.

"Ah, my little sweet," said the Emperor, his voice a hoarse croak. "You look so much like her today."

He meant Lana's mother, of course, whom he'd loved in his youth. He'd once been a handsome komodo-Kind, though looking at him now, this was hard to believe. When he lifted a clawed hand to stroke Lana's cheek, she managed not to flinch.

"Thank you, Your Highness," she said.

The Emperor lowered his hand with a sigh. "So honest and true. Unlike so many others in this city. All out for themselves."

As he spoke, he frowned at someone approaching.

Lana turned discreetly to see a middle-aged lizard-Kind ascending the stage. Her neck was adorned with gold bands, and she wore robes adorned with jewels. On her head, she wore an exotic headdress studded with precious stones. With clothes chosen to express her wealth, she looked more like a merchant than a courtier. A human followed just behind her. He was similarly dressed in expensive silks, so not a servant – more likely a trusted advisor. Both swept towards them. Lana noticed that Bart whispered something to Shahn as the pair passed them.

The lady's eyes sparkled with intelligence and familiarity. She bowed to the Emperor, but to Lana's great surprise, it wasn't the Emperor she addressed.

"My dearest Lana," she said. "So *pleased* to see you again."

Lana was caught off guard. "I'm sorry, good lady, I don't believe we've met."

"I suppose you wouldn't remember," said the woman. "You were but a small girl when I last came to the Burrows. My name is Florenz, sister to your poor father."

"Goodness!" said Lana. "My mother never mentioned you."

Florenz's mouth twisted. "No, perhaps she wouldn't. Well, no matter. I'm pleased the family's reputation has recovered sufficiently that we can *all* return to the city." She nodded towards the Emperor. "With the consent of Your Highness, of course."

The Emperor, who'd begun devouring a pile of bloody flesh served on a golden plate, nodded his absent-minded approval. Then he indicated for his bearers to carry him further on to the stage. The crowd began to applaud again.

Now that she'd had a moment to think about it, Lana wondered if she did vaguely recall Florenz visiting once, back when her father was alive.

"Such a terrible shame about your mother," said the woman. "She lost her mind, but in the eyes of the Court we *all* lost favour. No matter how unfairly. I warned my brother about the dangers of marrying into the Shadowscale brood, but love often conquers wisdom."

Lana recognised a cutting remark when she heard one, even when it was uttered in a friendly tone, but she forced herself to remain civil. If she was to be a serious candidate for the throne, she'd need to learn to hold her tongue and practise diplomacy.

"Clearly exile has done little to damage *your* fortunes, Lady Florenz." Lana gestured to the jewelled robes.

Florenz smiled. "Indeed. I was forced to make my own. I retreated to the Ruby Isle, to trade in spices and precious metals. Lucrative ventures, both. No doubt there are those in the city who would baulk at dealing with humans, but such silly prejudices only stand in the way of profit. Don't you agree?"

"Actually, I do," said Lana, "though profit alone should not be the only reason to move beyond old prejudices." She nodded at Florenz's human companion. "We must also consider our principles."

They were interrupted by the arrival of Shahn. "I love your headdress!" she told Florenz.

"Sister!" said Lana. "It's rude to interrupt."

"Ah, so you are my other niece," said Florenz. "The lovely Shahn. And don't you look delight—" The horn blew again, cutting off her words. "Oh, the ceremony is about to commence. I very much hope we will have time to talk later?"

"I look forward to it," said Lana, while thinking exactly the opposite. But she would have to make time. This aunt was obvious extremely wealthy. Her support would be useful. On the other hand, if Florenz was plotting something, then Lana needed to find out what it was.

Silash, the tall and thin lizard-Kind Court Speaker, stood at the front of the stage beside the Emperor's litter, to address the crowd.

"Greetings, subjects of Whitestone," he said, "and welcome to this grand occasion." He swept an arm towards the two new statues, both still covered with cloth tied down at ground level. "Soon you shall see the latest works commissioned by our Emperor in honour of his reign." The crowd, urged on by stewards, greeted these words with another round of cheering. "And yet," continued Silash, 'this is a sad day too. For the time soon approaches when our revered Lord Highness will step down from the throne he has occupied for many glorious years. When he will offer his crown to a chosen successor. Of course, the transition of power is never an easy time." His voice deepened, and he set his face in a concerned grimace. "This is the case now, perhaps, more than ever."

The crowd hushed. Lana, too, found herself focused on his every word. These days in Whitestone, politics was present in every action and gesture. She should have known a schemer like the Court Speaker would never miss a chance to push his interests. Not with the Emperor's abdication so close. She wondered what he was going to say next.

"The threat from the human rebels is *growing*," Silash went on. "Each day our scouts bring us news of their movements. They are like vermin gathering beneath our floorboards, eating away at our foundations. They *hate* us. They wish to destroy our way of life. They tell each other stories of bygone times when they ruled the Kind, murdering and controlling us."

The crow let out a round of hissing and booing. The Court Speaker knew his audience well.

"He's good at this, isn't he?" muttered Florenz. "Not that he actually knows a *thing* about the rebels' movements, of course."

Lana didn't respond. Not that she disagreed. Silash was all talk and no substance. A rabble-rouser and nothing more. But to openly criticise Silash was tantamount to criticising the Emperor himself – a dangerous and seditious act. Florenz took a tremendous risk in even whispering such a thing. Lana had to wonder why she'd do so.

"They would see every one of us killed or enslaved," Silash continued. "Do not be complacent! You need look no further than the rebel attack at Skin-Grave to see what villainy we face. Our dear Arch Protector Malachai – *may the Creator bless him* – met the threat there, and he paid the price. His grievous injuries rob us of his council when we most need it." His eyes rested coldly on Lana, as if he blamed her for Malachai's condition. "Meanwhile, across the kingdom, the rebels ceaselessly build their armies. They tell fond stories of days long ago when *we* were second-class citizens. They dabble with ancient dark magic. They scheme on ways to wipe the Kind from the kingdoms!"

"They must be stopped!" a lizard-Kind near the front of the crowd shouted.

"We must destroy them!" someone else shouted from the back. "We must kill them all!"

Silash was whipping the crowd into a frenzy. Impressive, in a way. Though Lana had to wonder why. This was supposed to be a joyous occasion to unveil the statues she'd worked so hard on. The Court Speaker had turned this commemoration of the Emperor's rule into something more like a political rally. The spectators were shouting curses and waving their arms in dismay.

"But fear not," Silash shouted. "My brood has thousands of soldiers at our disposal, and I do not fear to use them to protect us. To protect all Kind! I will meet the human threat with brutal, decisive action, the like of which has not been seen for generations!"

So that was his game. *He's making a bid for power, right beneath the nose of the Emperor.*

Beside Lana, Florenz scoffed. "Silash has no armies," she said. "He has a poorly trained rabble who'd rather drink wine and gamble than go into battle. Trust me, Lana, I have everything that matters – money, armour and weapons. You have will have the backing of all my resources in the upcoming election."

Lana looked at her aunt, trying to cover her

surprise. "Thank you, my lady. That's reassuring indeed."

She was careful not to seem too excited. She remembered her mother's lessons about courtly behaviour. You had to be able to dissemble, and to lie with gestures as well as words. Two things were certain: she'd need this aunt's support in the coming intrigues, and she couldn't trust her in the least.

"Now," continued the Court Speaker, raising an arm towards the veiled statues, "I present to you these gifts from the Emperor himself!"

The ropes fastening the statues' covers were cut, and the great drapes fell away. The crowd gasped in astonishment as Lana's works were revealed. The first statue depicted the Emperor himself, or at least the handsome komodo-Kind of two decades earlier when he'd ascended the throne. Even with that as a model, Lana had embellished his figure considerably. The statue stood in magnificent armour that the bloated reality wouldn't currently be able to even stand upright in. He held a curved blade above his head as if leading the Kind into a battle. In truth, such a battle had never taken place.

Impressive as the Emperor's statue was, Lana sensed the attention of the crowd was focused on the second of her two sculptures, and her heart filled with pride. This was the majestic form of Elrith the Living Shadow: Lana's ancestor, the first empress, who had united the Four Kingdoms so long ago. The imperious figure actually loomed slightly taller than the Emperor's, which was an entirely intentional decision on Lana's part. The statue's face was fixed in a fierce yet protective expression, but the most stunning element was the statue's arm, which pointed over the crowd. The first empress had been shadow-blessed just like Lana. The same magical shadow that flickered over the statue's arm also danced along the right side of Lana's own body.

The effect was powerful and clear.

The crowd cheered, but it took a moment for Lana to realise a slow chant was building too.

She felt a blush rising to her cheeks. They were saying *her* name.

"La-na, La-na, La-na!"

Silash, she noticed, was scowling, but Bart sidled up beside her. "I think you should say something," he said. "This is your moment."

"I can't," she said, suddenly over-awed. Then more loudly, so the Emperor could hear. "This is the Emperor's day."

The komodo-Kind on his palanquin nodded

to her, giving his permission. Ignoring Silash's disapproval, Lana took a few steps to position herself more centrally on the stage. The Court Speaker moved aside, still glaring at her. Almost at once, the crowd fell silent. Was it her imagination, or had their expressions changed? Before, they'd seemed suspicious of her shadow, but now they looked something closer to intrigued. Even foolish old Bart had sensed it – this was her chance. She cleared her throat.

"Behold!" she said. Her voice carried on the warm air, louder than she expected. "Behold my ancestor, Elrith, the Shadowscale Empress, taking her rightful place in the pageant of our *greatest* rulers." *That should please the Emperor.* "Elrith, who united the Four Kingdoms. Elrith, who kept us safe by crushing the human nations that had dominated us for so long!"

This brought a spontaneous roar from the crowd, with no encouragement needed from the stewards. But from the corner of her eye, Lana noted that Jun looked irritated. Didn't she understand? If Lana was to stand any chance of ascending to the throne, she had to play the game. If the people hated humans, then she had to pretend she hated them even more. Any inkling she was a sympathiser would end her campaign as sharply as an axe-blade to the neck.

"I know that many of you view my shadow with unease," she said. "My family's recent history – my mother's curse – is no secret. But remember that Elrith too was shadow-blessed. Our shadow is a noble trait, a gift from the Creator himself, and I mean to use it in the service of the Kind."

"Bravo!" shouted the Emperor. "Bravo!" He sat up straighter on his cushions and began to clap. The other courtiers on stage joined in dutifully. The crowd echoed this with passion. Shahn began to whoop and Uncle Bart brought his hands together with enthusiasm. Lana bowed to the people, then turned back to bow to the Emperor too. As she did, she caught Florenz's gaze. Her aunt applauded with everyone else and gave her a complimentary nod. Only Silash seemed unmoved. He left the stage, no doubt to lick his wounds somewhere more private.

Then came a shout from below, and not a happy one. "Hey! Stop!" someone called out.

Lana turned to the outburst and saw a steward stumbling and pointing. From the ranks of spectators broke a single human figure. A young man. He carried a curved sword in each hand and wore a gleaming breastplate across his chest.

"Stop him!" cried Bart.

But the boy was agile, and in a single bound he leapt to the edge of the stage. He set his eyes on the Emperor and raised his blades. The litter-bearers on either side of the palanquin were unarmed, and they backed away. The assembled nobles and courtiers too recoiled from the attacker, and the guards were too far away.

The Emperor was defenceless.

Lana threw off her cloak, and shadow erupted over her tunic beneath. She threw an arm towards the statue of her ancestor, willing the marble to move. At once, it did. Life flowed into the stone, and Elrith lifted a foot from her pedestal like a living giant. The human assassin skidded to a halt, tipping back his head to take in the shocking sight of the colossal, shadow-wreathed woman. He seemed rooted to the spot as Lana brought the foot right down on top of him. He disappeared in a crash of wood and rubble as the stage collapsed beneath the weight of the marble foot.

For a few seconds, there was silence. Lana stood with her arm extended, tendrils of shadow linking her to the statue of Elrith, which had frozen into its murderous pose.

Finally, the guards reached the Emperor. The courtiers descended a moment later, smoothing their clothes as they checked on the ruler's wellbeing. Silash scurried back to the stage, fussing at his leader's side, but the Emperor shoved him away. He ordered his litter-bearers to get him safely back into the palace, then pointed to Lana.

"Bring her too!"

Lana fell into step behind the retinue. Jun hurried to her side, and Shahn followed close behind her.

"That was incredible, sister!" Shahn said. "You saved the Emperor's life!"

Lana nodded. "Go straight home with Uncle," she said. "I'll be back at the house as soon as I can."

She was quickly swept up alongside the parade of courtiers trailing after the Emperor on his way back through the palace gates. Stewards formed a double column through the crowd, keeping the people at bay. As Lana walked through the gauntlet, many called out her name in adulation.

"You know," said Jun, leaning close to her side, "there was something rather strange about the way that assassin appeared from nowhere."

"Oh yes?" said Lana innocently.

Jun caught her arm, slowing her down. She looked cross. "If I didn't know you better, I'd think you used your shadow magic to create him, just so you could destroy him."

Lana gave her friend a meaningful glare. "That would be cunning indeed," she said. "But perhaps keep your voice down."

Jun kept her grip on Lana's arm. "I know you want to ingratiate yourself with the people, but at what cost? Was inventing a *human* assassin necessary? Fomenting hatred of my people will only lead to more purges."

Lana tugged her arm free. "Once I'm in power, Jun – there'll be no more purges. That I promise you."

Jun looked unconvinced and stalked off.

Lana understood her concerns, but Jun was an idealist. She didn't appreciate how cut-throat the court could be, with so many clamouring for power. Lana had to use every tool at her disposal if she was going to be noticed. And if that meant taking advantage of anti-human prejudice, so be it.

"That was incredible," said a gecko-Kind as he walked past, confirming Lana's thoughts perfectly. "May the Creator bless the Shadowscale line."

Lana nodded her thanks.

But as she joined the retinue trailing into the Emperor's quarters, she did feel a twinge of unease. The plan had worked, but several details about the shadow assassin concerned her. Mainly the fact that he hadn't appeared at all as she envisaged. She'd intended him to be a rough man of the forest armed with a hatchet. Yet he'd been a boy, with twin swords and a finely wrought breastplate.

Which left her with some unnerving questions.

What did it mean that she couldn't trust her shadow magic to create exactly what she intended?

And why was Slayer so deeply occupying her thoughts?

7

AN UNCERTAIN MEETING

"Drop your swords," said the tribesman holding the dagger to Halima's neck.

With the death-song ringing in his blood, a part of Jonas longed to fight on. He knew he could cleave the attacker in half with a single blow. But could he do so before the tribesman slaughtered Halima? There was a time when this wouldn't have mattered. Without hesitation, he would have brought death upon everyone in range. But the ancient golden breastplate softened the song of death.

More ambushers emerged from the trees, including those he'd injured. One was bleeding from both nostrils and the other clutched the bleeding stump where his hand had been. One of his fellows had wrapped the seeping flesh in cloth and stanched the flow of blood with a tourniquet.

"He cut my hand off!" he screamed in rage and pain. "Let me kill him."

"I'll take the other if you so much as think of it," said Jonas.

"There'll be no killing yet," said the one with Halima. "Not until Resala says so. Throw down your blades, young man."

For Halima's sake, Jonas knew he had to do as he'd been told. He cast his swords to the ground, where the man with the broken nose retrieved them. Still, he kept a wary eye on the one-handed archer. *Former* archer, he supposed.

"Who is Resala?" he said.

"You'll see soon enough," said the tribesman. "Darwa, bind his hands."

The tribesmen led them north-east.

Their captors tugged the ropes that bound them, leading them through the trees like cattle. But Jonas was no longer afraid. If these had been common bandits, they'd have already slaughtered him and Halima by now and taken anything they had worth stealing. In any event, they were heading in roughly the same direction Jonas had intended to travel. Still, he wished he could have sensed Seth's presence nearby, just in case the situation turned nasty. He was fairly sure the ghost-wyvern was nowhere in the vicinity.

Where is he? What's he doing?

As the sun tracked across the sky, they trekked through remote mountain valleys, crossed streams and clambered over boulders. If there was a trail here, Jonas couldn't see it. Halima had gone even more silent than she'd been before, and Jonas used the time to appraise the tribesfolk more closely.

The leader had long black hair tied in a knot and wore buffalo hide. Jonas was fairly sure the dagger he carried was made of redsteel. This was a rare and expensive metal, far lighter and stronger than regular steel. Jonas assumed the weapon was stolen, as only Kind were permitted to carry such a precious thing. Most such weapons were reserved for the Emperor's Own.

The man who'd lost his hand was shaven-headed but for a small ridge at the front. He was darker skinned than the others and dressed in a tunic that left his tattooed arms bare. The woman who'd tied Jonas's hands wore pantaloons, wide at the thighs but tight around her ankles. She was very pale, her nose and cheeks sprinkled with freckles.

Their appearances were almost comically different. They were clearly from different tribes yet were working together nonetheless.

When the group traversed a narrow pass, the landscape opened up to reveal a small lake situated below a horseshoe of snow-capped mountains pocked with cavern openings. Some of the tunnel openings looked as if they'd been hollowed out by hand. Smoke drifted from firepits, near which people stood to watch Jonas's approach. A few goats and hens scurried around.

As they got closer, more tribesfolk emerged from the caves. Again they seemed to belong to vastly different groups, their attire and appearance indicating they came from every corner of the Four Kingdoms. The one thing they had in common, though, was the type of weapons they carried. Spears, swords, axes – they all had the dull scarlet gleam of redsteel.

There was no way they could have stolen such an incredible trove of arms. And they couldn't have made them themselves: red iron wasn't mined from anywhere in the mountains. The only known deposits were in the lands far to the east. The redsteel itself was only smelted by a special guild of craftsmen on the Ruby Isle.

Someone has armed these people. Someone powerful.

The tribesfolk watched sullenly as Jonas and Halima were paraded through the camp. Soon they reached a large cave mouth carved with runic shapes. A single figure emerged. She was older than Jonas, but not by much, and powerfully built. Her hair was braided down to her waist. Where she wasn't dressed in furs, her skin was covered in tattoos. Blue markings decorated even her cheeks, jaw and forehead. The spindly shapes etched onto her reminded Jonas of something, though he couldn't quite say what. In her hand she gripped a three-sectioned flail made of redsteel.

"What have you found, Trog?" she asked.

"Two humans," replied the ponytailed captor. He threw down Jonas's curved swords. "The boy can fight."

The woman looked at the tribesman who was missing a hand. "So I see." She fixed her eyes on the swords, then on Jonas. "What is your tribe?"

She spoke in a strange manner. Her teeth seemed to bite at the words, making a staccato clicking sound.

"We are fugitives from the swamplands," said

Jonas, thinking quickly. "Insect-Kind attacked our village, but we fled. We're trying to get to Anoros."

The woman frowned. "Then you're heading by a curious route," she said. "Not to mention a dangerous one, if it's insect-Kind you fear. It's much quicker and safer to head past Whitestone or up the coast."

"We got a little lost," put in Halima. "Perhaps you could help us with directions?"

The tribe leader smiled. "The swamplands, you say? Your accent is strange for those parts. And it doesn't at all match his." She pointed the flails at Jonas. "Perhaps we should torture you to find out where you're really from?"

"I volunteer," said the newly one-handed man.

The death-song flared through Jonas's veins, showing him his demise in a dozen ways.

He rolls for his sword and his hand finds the hilt, but in the same second, the woman's flail caves in his skull.

He strained helplessly at the cords on his wrist as he scanned the cliffs surrounding them.

Where in the name of the Creator is Seth?

"You're searching for your monster, I think?" said the woman. Now she had Jonas's attention. "I knew who you were the moment I saw your blades, Slayer. You are the cursed one, who slaughtered his tribe and does the bidding of the Gaoler. This girl must be destined for the Pinnacles. But tell me, where are the famed manacles that bind you to Grashkor?"

Jonas shared a glance with Halima. It seemed pointless to continue any deception.

"She is not a prisoner," he said. "And I am no longer a bounty hunter."

"No one escapes the Pinnacles," the woman said with a frown.

"They do now," Halima declared, not just to the woman, but to the crowd assembled around them. "When Jonas decided not to deliver me to the Pinnacles, Grashkor chased us down. He sought to kill Jonas in punishment, but it was Jonas who killed him. The Gaoler is dead."

The tribesmen turned to each other, muttering in astonishment.

"Impressive, I suppose," the woman said. "But in the end, just another chapter in your blood-soaked legend."

"You have the advantage over us," Jonas told her. "For we don't have the slightest idea who you are."

"My name is Resala," said the woman. "Where is it you and your *companion* are really going? The rebel stronghold, perhaps?"

Jonas didn't reply. Nor did Halima, though her

eyes were fierce.

"I'm afraid you may be too late," continued Resala. "My airborne scouts have located their base – it is protected by a magical gateway, but we'll find a way through soon enough. Then we'll strike."

"Wait," said Halima in confusion. "You're human. Would you want to fight the rebels? They're on your side; they're enemies of the Emperor. They seek the freedom of all humankind."

"And what do you mean, *airborne scouts*?" asked Jonas.

Resala sighed. "Do you really think the world is so simple as humans and Kind at war?" she said. "Do you really believe peace will reign if one side prevails?" She raised her voice now, so that more of the tribespeople could hear. "I have made alliances with the Kind *and* with human tribes. I have fought those who stood in my way and proved my worth to lead. Under my leadership, we work *together* to ensure our survival and our freedom from the tyranny of human and Kind alike." She raised her flail in the air, and the people all around let out a roar of approval. Resala lowered her weapon and her voice. "The question is, will you join us?"

"Do we have a choice?" asked Jonas.

Resala shrugged. "Death is always an option. You

should know that better than anyone."

Jonas glanced at Halima, who gave a tiny shake of her head. All around them, the crowd was silent, waiting to see what he would say. But it was Halima who spoke first.

"We choose a duel," she said. "A one-on-one fight. If we prevail, you must grant us our freedom."

Resala grinned. "And why should I accept this offer?"

"Because you're not a coward," said Halima. "Because you claim to be able to lead these people. Trial by combat is the way of the tribes, as you know."

Jonas admired Halima's quick thinking.

"If I win," said Resala, "I want his pretty armour."

"If you win, you have every right to do with us, and our possessions, as you wish," said Halima.

"Very well," Resala said. "Of the two of you, I assume Slayer will be your champion."

Jonas stepped forward. "Of course. But I don't want to kill you."

"Me?" Resala chuckled. "Oh, you won't be fighting me," she said. "I name my sister Kykyra as my champion." She turned towards the cave mouth from which she'd emerged and let out a series of chittering, clicking sounds. It was a language Jonas was familiar with, though he'd never dreamed he'd hear a human speak it.

Tribesmen backed away from the cave entrance as a huge creature scuttled from the shadows. It was an enormous beetle-Kind, the size of a carthorse. Its thorax was protected by redsteel armour. The forged plates were engraved with similar markings to Resala's tattoos. Now Jonas realised where he'd seen such patterns before – these were the war-emblems of the barbarian insect-Kind clans.

"That's your *sister*?" said Halima.

"These lands were the insect-Kind's territory before humans ever set foot here," said Resala. "All the Quarg Mountains once belonged to Quargos, god of the insect-Kind. As a baby, I was left at the sacred Nara Lake, where the sangwar trees were felled. I had been given as an offering to the insect-Kind, but instead of killing me, they raised me among their own young."

Now that the giant beetle-Kind had stepped closer, Jonas saw her legs were strapped with redsteel blades. The creature let out a chittering sound of her own and set her antennae twitching. From the rock openings above, more insects burst forth on wings. As they launched themselves into the air, the sky turned dark behind their swarm. They descended into a circular formation around Jonas and Kykyra. The human tribesmen were pressed close too, all eager for bloodshed.

"It's not too late to change your mind," said Resala. "If you give me the armour and swear allegiance to our cause, you can both live."

Jonas's eyes were fixed on the armoured beetle-Kind, already looking for vulnerable points he could attack.

"Fighting against both the Emperor and the human rebels will mean endless war, not peace," he told Resala.

He was Slayer, and fighting would always be a part of his destiny. But now he had a choice about who to fight for. *What* to fight for. Now that he could finally make his destiny his own, it was his responsibility to make the right choices. Everything about Resala and her alliance between insect-Kind and the tribesman felt wrong.

"It's conquer or be conquered," said Resala. "Now take off your breastplate and prepare to fight."

"No!" said Halima. "That's not fair."

"It is the item wagered, and so it cannot play a role in the combat," said Resala. "Take it off or die on the spot."

Jonas did as he was told. He unfastened the straps

and handed the armour to Trog. "Don't worry," he said to Halima. "I fight better without it."

And it was true.

Without the breastplate dampening the death-song, he would fight with all the strength, violence and savagery he was capable of.

A good thing too, he thought as the clacking mandibles of the insectoid warrior came close. Because to stand a chance of surviving this, he was going to need every advantage he could get.

THE LOST CITY

*T*he Lost City was a place of ancient power.

Magic flowed everywhere. It drifted along subtle currents of the air and radiated from the very cobbles under Gael's feet as the Reader led him through warrens of alleyways and streets. The canyons of fine buildings breathed it out and Gael breathed it in.

The feel of it made him long for the Netherplane, from which he'd emerged so very long ago.

He was the last of the Gateway Keepers. The last of those entrusted to keep the portals between the worlds safe and in order. Many times, he'd been tempted to return to the place of his origin, but something always stopped him. Even in those long centuries when he'd made himself distant to the affairs of this world and the perpetual struggles between humans and Kind, he'd never quite been able to bring himself to leave.

There was something just so endlessly *fascinating* about this world and its people.

What better example than this place, the Lost City itself? He had to admit, it had exceeded his every expectation. This was no squalid rebel stronghold populated by desperate renegades, but a prospering city. Like Skin-Grave, its concentric walls were stout and strong, well buttressed and defended with arrow slits. As Gael and the Reader wound through the streets, the ground rose ever higher until he found himself breathing hard with the effort of walking.

The gatehouses they frequently encountered were manned by guards in towers high above, carrying crossbows, and by armoured soldiers at street level, wielding halberds and pikes. All bore the elaborate "H" of New Havanthya on their breastplates. Murder holes for boiling oil or rocks gaped above, ready to deliver death on any who'd seek to enter the city by force.

"Fine defences," Gael remarked to the Reader. "Though I certainly wouldn't like to be here if they were ever needed."

These words settled on him as they made their way onwards. With every turn, with every new sight, Gael became more certain of something incredible: that they weren't new sights all. That he had in fact been here before, centuries ago. Indeed, not only had he seen these formidable defences in action, he'd already witnessed them being pushed beyond their limits.

Suddenly he could see it all again as it had been an age ago. The streets were filled with bodies. Stray dogs and rats feasted on the carrion dead. Every building not aflame was in ruins from the Kind siege engines that had rained destruction from beyond the wrecked walls.

Gael had been here when this city was sacked, and he marvelled at this sudden memory of the place. Perhaps this was a city so secret and so very magic that it somehow invited forgetfulness.

As for those gruesome memories, the city couldn't be more different now. The buildings had been repaired; the sewers had been covered over. Humans were going about their daily lives, carrying baskets of fresh produce or wheeling carts through the streets. Children played with a ball in a courtyard around a sparkling fountain. In one square, a small cattle auction was under way. Hammers rang out from the blacksmiths' forges, while at a dressmaker's, women unloaded bolts of cloth.

"You're impressed," said the Reader as they stopped to let a milkmaid pass bearing a yoke and two overflowing buckets.

"But not surprised. Humans are remarkably resilient," said Gael.

"We have been reclaiming the culture that was kept from us," the Reader said as she continued walking. "What our engineers couldn't remember, we translated from ancient scrolls in the Tower of Forbidden Knowledge and from the archives under the Lost City. This will become the capital of New Havanthya. A safe haven for humans against the Kind in Anoros."

"If the Emperor learns of this place, he will raze it to the ground," said Gael.

The Reader turned to him with deadly seriousness. "And we will defend it to the last man or woman."

"That's the most likely outcome," Gael agreed. "When you've lived as long as me, you get used to seeing even the noblest of hopes die."

"I'm not sure you believe that," the Reader said.

When they reached yet another formidable gate, the Reader spoke to the guard. He gave a cry for it to be opened. As the heavy doors swung back,

Gael saw they'd reached the central complex of the city. The keep was a solid tower of thick stone. Its battlements above were lined with giant crossbows and catapults, clearly aimed at repelling airborne invaders or taking out siege engines beyond the walls.

More memories returned to Gael.

In the age of Thom, a palace had stood here. This was where Hugo and his queen, Haroha, had reigned from their thrones during their peaceful fifty-year rule. Now only the central keep remained. Gael found himself drawn to a low doorway.

"It's this way," the Reader called to him. But Gael ignored her, his feet tugged by the past. "Those are just old storerooms," she said.

Gael entered the doorway anyway and shuffled down some steps. From his cloak, he drew a glowstone. He rubbed it between his hands so it would throw soft golden light around. At the bottom of the steps, he found himself in a low cellar, the ceiling of which was supported by arches of stone. Crates lay here and there, and racks were loaded with jars of oil or wine. The Reader arrived behind him.

"What are you *doing*?" she asked. "We have places to be."

Gael walked towards one of the arches. The light from the glowstone picked out the pockmarks on the stones. Among these was one particular brick, a slightly different shade from the rest. "I've been here before," he told her. "And don't forget – doorways are my speciality."

Reaching out, he laid his fingers against the brick and pushed. A clunking of metal came from the far side of the wall, and with a thump, the whole alcove moved a finger's breadth inwards, releasing a puff of dust from its edges. The Reader gasped.

Gael pushed on the left side and the stone door swung open on hinges surprisingly well-oiled. There were more steps, these ones winding downwards in a spiral.

"It's my turn to show you around," Gael told his companion.

He led the way, his glowstone's light creeping ahead into the shadows as they descended. The air here was cool and damp. At the bottom, a passageway flanked by columns led to a wide doorway. Beyond this, they came to a large chamber. Gael rubbed the stone again to give out more illumination, and he smiled as the glow caught on grand carved sarcophagi.

"What is this place?" asked the Reader.

"They called it the Gallery of Tombs," said Gael. "Only the greatest heroes of their age were laid to rest here." He walked into the chamber and lifted the glowstone so its light shone on the faces of the statues lining the walls. "There's Thom," he said, nodding towards the grizzled old warrior carrying his famous shield set with relics of the old-Kind. "Next to him is his father Thaladon, who was slain by Malvale." He moved the glowstone further. "That one is the first Master of the Kind, Thanner." Gael looked at the Reader. "One day, Jonas's likeness will join them."

The Reader stared at the noble carvings. "So you believe."

"Each of the warriors entombed here once walked the Master's Road. Jonas has already taken his first steps on the same journey. It is fated."

The Reader pointed at Thanner. "I have been studying the *Chronicles of Havanthya*. The ancient stories tell of how Thanner was corrupted by dark magic. There are many stories of great human warriors who turned to evil."

A uneasy feeling stirred in Gael's chest, and he lowered the glowstone so that it cast long shadows upon the Reader's face.

He knew the Reader spoke the truth. Humans

were as prone to corruption as any other being. Jonas had been through terrible events. His trials and losses and burdens could be the ingredients for the very greatness required of him. Yet . . .

The Reader's words had snagged an inkling of memory. The older you are, the more there is to forget, but something about this fragment of recollection struck Gael as important. There was another story from long ago that he felt with some urgency he must remember.

He had to get out into the open air again, so he could think more clearly. "Come," he said. "Let's continue with your tour."

"Careful with that," said Gael as a servant brought in his chest of instruments. "Over there, on the bureau, please."

The Reader had found fine quarters for him on the top floor of the Keep, with arched windows looking to the south. The city thrived below, and encampments and farmland sprawled beyond its outer walls. More humans had already arrived than the city could hold.

And all of them drawn here by the promise of the future. All of them here to chase the dream of

New Havanthya.

Their hope. Their innocence. This was humanity's flaw.

But, taking it all in, Gael realised that it was also the very thing that had brought him to their side. Their mad, ferocious refusal to be vanquished. Their ability to look doom in the eye and somehow be stronger for it.

He began to set up his instruments on the windowsill to monitor the magical conditions. Beneath his window, far below, a little human girl chased a kitten, giggling and calling its name – "Trillia! Come back here!"

He watched the cat and the girl dart into an alley, and his mood turned dark. Did she know how fragile her existence was? The Lost City was like a bubble waiting to be popped. The sole way into this secret haven was concealed for now, but the Emperor's agents would locate it eventually. It was inevitable.

When the Emperor attacked, this sanctuary would quickly turn into a slaughter-yard. There'd be no more laughter then. Only screams.

Gael sighed. This was one of the rare occasions when he felt the burden of his many centuries of life. But it only lasted for a moment, and he soon found himself smiling. Hope still remained in his heart. Perhaps some of humanity had rubbed off on him after all these years.

Yes, Gael would continue to help them.

Even if he didn't always provide the help they thought they wanted.

There was a knock at the door, and another servant stood there, holding in his arms a single heavy tome. He was breathing heavily from the long walk up the stairs.

"You requested this?" he panted.

"Very good," said Gael. "On the table, please."

The servant deposited the leather-bound book and scurried out.

Gael went to the table to examine the tome. This volume of the *Chronicles* was a copy, rather than an original, and he hoped the scribes had been diligent. After blowing the dust off the cover, he opened it. Some of the calligraphy left something to be desired, but the writing was clear enough. He flicked through the pages, looking for the particular tale that had suddenly come to his mind in the Gallery of Tombs. Much of the early sections concerned the legend of Thom and his upbringing. There was no way to say for sure if it was all true. The bit about his wooden sword seemed particularly unlikely. But sometimes, exact truth wasn't the point. The message of a story was the most important thing.

Gael sped through several more pages about Thom's early battles to free the old-Kind from Malvale's enchantments. These sections had originally been written by Ajuro, the wise wizard of King Hugo's court. They were written in the language of old Havanthya and Gael was out of practice, so it took some time for him to get going. Soon he found the part he sought: the part that the Reader had reminded him of when she'd spoken of the corruption of some humans of the past. This was a tale of a human boy who fell under Malvale's influence. A boy who happened to share the name of Jonas's ghost-wyvern.

Seth.

The *Chronicles'* entry on this matter was simple and dry, relating only the barest facts.

"The dark wizard Malvale sought to corrupt more Kind to his evil ways. He sent his warrior Seth to steal the baby twin dragons Vedrios and Krimios and corrupt them with dark magic. Vedrios was green and Krimios was red, and they had but recently hatched. Seth only succeeded in stealing Vedrios and placing a curse on him. Thom and his companion Helenya were sent by Dalthek to find the young dragon, and eventually broke the curse

and brought Vedrios to safety."

Gael read on, but the *Chronicles* contained little else useful. The matching names of the ancient boy and the wyvern *might* just have been a coincidence, of course, but something about it had hooked in his thoughts. It was lodged there, tugging at him like a warning.

But a warning of what?

He yawned and closed the book with a thump. It had been a long day indeed – of travel, of debate and of surprises. He should save his energy for teleporting.

He plucked the jewelled beetle from his voluminous sleeve and held it on his palm. "Show me Whitestone again, Felix. Show me the attack."

The beetle's golden wings became a blur as it hovered above his hand then projected its footage in the centre of the room. Gael watched the events in the white city and the ceremony surrounding the unveiling of the imperial statues. The Shadowscale girl was making quite a name for herself, saving the Emperor's life like that. But Gael wasn't fooled by the illusion of the assassin. Lana might present herself as the shy newcomer, but there was no doubt she was quite cunning and ambitious.

Such a girl might be useful, if he could ensure her

motives aligned with his.

He took the purple jewel from his chest, ready to open a portal.

Though he was tired, he decided it was time to pay Lana a visit.

9

TRIAL BY COMBAT

*W*ithout the golden breastplate, the death-song roared inside Jonas's ears.

The world narrowed to his opponent: Kykyra, the giant beetle-Kind sister of Resala who loomed high above him.

The Swords of What Was and What Will Be were almost weightless in Jonas's hands, ready to slash and stab and taste her flesh. Any flesh. He tried to hold his violence in check, knowing that if he gave in to the seductive song, it wouldn't only be the beetle-Kind who died that day. Everyone in the crowds surrounding them, looking on and baying for the duel to begin, might meet his blade.

Kykyra stamped her six legs and scoured the

ground with her horns, throwing up a curtain of dust.

"I will enjoy pulling apart your limbs, Slayer," she said. Her words were delivered with the strange clicking of her mandibles.

Jonas fought against the urge to launch himself at her. There was still a chance conflict could be avoided.

"I'm not your enemy," he replied.

"Your tribe treated insect-Kind like savages," said Kykyra. "All we ever did was fight for survival."

"Those were the actions of others, now gone," said Jonas. "You and I have no quarrel."

"We have seen your sort before. As long as you live, you will seek vengeance and power," said Kykyra. "Only with your death will my people be safe. Throw down your swords, and I will make it quick."

Jonas saw there was no point in arguing further. The humans and insect-Kind around them had begun to chant Kykyra's name. She could no more back out of this than he could. He spun his blades in wide arcs. "Come and get them," he said through gritted teeth.

The beetle-Kind surged forward with alarming speed. Jonas saw his death at once.

He trips backwards, scrambling, but too slow. A foot pins his chest, breaking his breastbone. The mandibles sink into his face, crushing his skull like a bird's egg.

Jonas flipped himself sideways to land in a crouch and deliver a strike. It skimmed off a redsteel-armoured leg in a shower of sparks. The crowd roared. Jonas adjusted his body and swung with the other blade, this time at the small gap where the armour ended and the joint was exposed. Black gore sprayed across the faces of Trog and his companions as one of Kykyra's legs was severed.

The beetle-Kind barely seemed to notice as she rounded on him. She shook her head and caught him with a horn, hurling him off his feet. He turned his body in mid-air and tumbled across the ground to roll back to his feet.

From the edge of his vision, he noticed that Resala looked worried at the sight of the insect leg on the ground. "Kill him!" she screamed.

Kykyra advanced again, this time more cautiously.

"Give up," said Jonas, still managing to hold the death-song at bay. "I don't wish to hurt you."

Someone shoved him from behind, throwing him off balance. He stumbled forwards then fell headlong, dropping one sword. Kykyra was on him in the flash of a moment. She stamped with a spiked foot, but he rolled away to avoid the strike. He deflected her second attack with his remaining blade. Then the beetle opened her mandibles and dived for him. Jonas's shoulder was caught in her sharp iron grip as she shook him from side to side, dragging his body back and forth through the dust. He gripped her armoured head for dear life until it felt like his bones were coming apart. When she paused for a split second, he jammed his fist into the eye socket of her helmet. He struck hard enough to make her buck away. When her mandibles released him, Jonas slammed into the ground and dropped his weapon. In his anger he let the death-song in. He could do nothing to stop it surging through his blood.

It felt *glorious*.

He picked up the nearest sword and slid beneath Kykyra's body. Raking the edge of his blade across her belly, he severed the clasps of her armour. She tried to crush him with her thorax, but he was too quick and danced away even as he landed his own blow. His blade whistled through a rear leg. Off balance, the insect-Kind collapsed on to her belly. As Jonas pivoted, he saw the faces of the astonished crowd. Their mouths hung open in shock, their eyes wide. It was a look he'd seen countless times.

You did not understand what I was . . .

. . . and now you will never forget.

He leapt on to the insect-Kind's back. With his free hand, he found the edge of her armour and ripped it away to expose her vulnerable flesh. The place where the thorax met her head parts would be the killing spot. He twisted the blade to brace its point against her neck. Resala opened her mouth to scream, but that wouldn't stop him. The death-song left no shred of pity.

He placed both hands on the hilt, ready to thrust it home . . .

Then a face in the screaming crowd caught his eye and stopped his blade.

A girl, watching from the very back. Among the writhing masses only she was motionless as she watched him. His cousin.

"Fran?"

Her eyes bored into his. They were filled with sorrow, as if he'd disappointed her. As if this was some childish game he was too old to play.

The bloodlust drained away in an instant. The death-song was silenced, and the crowd with it.

Standing astride the beetle-Kind's shell, he turned to Halima. For a moment, she looked so much like his cousin he could have sworn they were the same. When he glanced back to where Fran had stood just a second before, she was gone.

"Do you yield?" he asked Kykyra. His blade still rested against her neck.

"I do," clicked the wounded beetle. "You have bested me, Slayer."

Jonas pointed his sword at Resala. "And will you let us pass, unmolested, as you promised?"

Resala glowered, and the attention of her people turned towards her. "I honour my word," she said. "You are free to go, Slayer. While you are in our lands, no harm will befall you."

The sun was close to setting as they climbed the last few strides to the mountain pass. Jonas had kept his eyes peeled throughout their journey here. Firstly, because he didn't entirely trust Resala's promise. And secondly, because they had no idea what other threats might lie in wait along their path.

At least Halima herself was now armed as well. She carried a bow and quiver donated by Resala. A gift bestowed as they'd left, though Jonas remained unconvinced by the peace offering.

"Perhaps I should have killed her," he said.

"You cut off two of her legs," said Halima. "I think she got the message."

"I meant Resala," said Jonas. "She will attack the rebels as soon as she gets the chance."

"Perhaps," said the girl. "Now it's our job to be ready if she does." She paused. "How did you stop yourself, this time?"

"What do you mean?"

"One moment you were like a maniac. I saw your face, the way it was consumed with fury. It was as if you were a different person, Jonas. Then . . . well, it just went away. I know the golden breastplate helps you control the violence, but you weren't wearing it."

They had reached the pass and below them lay the plains of Anoros, dotted with swathes of forest. Along the distant horizon, a smudge of mountains, or perhaps sea. They gazed quietly at the vista.

"I saw my cousin again," said Jonas at last. "Like I did back at the camp."

"A ghost?"

"I don't know," Jonas sighed. "A spirit, I suppose. You look so much like her. I think . . ."

"What?"

"I wonder if you're connected somehow? The sangwar tree shows how past, present and future exist together. Perhaps you two share the same essence, or she's coming through you to me, trying to tell me something." Jonas closed his eyes, trying to fathom everything that had happened to him in the last few days.

"It might just be a coincidence that we look alike," said Halima.

"It's more," Jonas said. Of this much he was certain. "She never visited me until I found you. And it's not just your appearance. It's all so familiar – your personality, your mannerisms. I noticed it the moment we met."

"The Reader may have answers for you," said Halima. She hefted her bow and set an arrow to the string. "Helenya carried a bow too, you know," she said, smiling. "She saved Thom from certain death countless times, or so the storytellers claim. Do you suppose that has some grand deeper meaning, too?" she asked as she smiled at him.

Then suddenly she gasped and pivoted towards him. She drew the bow, the arrow pointing more in Jonas's direction than he'd prefer.

"Hey!" he said, jerking away instinctively. "Watch where you're pointing that thing!"

"Don't move!" she shouted, then her face creased into a scowl. "Oh – it's *you*!"

Jonas turned to see Seth sitting on a rocky outcrop ten paces away.

"I'd rather you didn't point it at me either," he said calmly.

Halima lowered the bow.

"Where've you *been*?" asked Jonas angrily.

"Yeah, we could have used some help earlier," added Halima. "You know – when we were almost *executed*."

Seth folded his wings and sighed. "I had some business in the east," he said, nodding towards the setting sun. The horizon was a dark, dusty strip.

"The Forbidden Lands?" said Jonas suspiciously. "What were you up to there?"

"Nothing good, I'd reckon," said Halima. "It's the realm of the ghost-Kind."

"I go there from time to time," said Seth, "to consult with my kin."

"Is that where you always go when you disappear?" asked Jonas.

"Among other places," said Seth blithely. "But listen, brother, there are answers there for you too. Come with me to the east."

"Answers about what?"

"About the past," said Seth. "About what happened to your tribe."

He's teasing me, thought Jonas. "If you know something, just tell me."

Seth shook his head. "No, that wouldn't be right. It's not so . . . simple. You must find out these things for yourself."

"You're really annoying, you know that?" said Halima.

Seth sneered at her. "Says the human leading him on a wild goose chase she calls *destiny*." He focused on Jonas. "I know we haven't been seeing eye to eye recently, but I promise you, you need to discover what I've learned. You won't regret it. Afterwards, you can go with this girl to her magical city. I won't stop you."

Jonas turned to Halima, who rolled her eyes. She pointed across the plains below, to a large area of forest. "The rebel stronghold is half a day's travel at most. We need to tell the Reader about Resala and her army."

"Can't you do that on your own?" asked Seth. "You don't need Jonas to hold your hand the *entire* way, do you?"

"These lands are dangerous," said Jonas. "We've already been ambushed once. No. I'm going with Halima. Once she's safely with her people, I can visit the Forbidden Lands."

Seth flapped his wings. His wound had healed already, Jonas noted. "Very well, Slayer," said the wyvern. "Have it your way. But do try not to get killed."

With that, he turned ghostly and flew away.

"Thank you," said Halima. "I don't trust him."

Jonas could only smile. "Neither do I, really. Come on, let's keep moving."

They descended from the pass and soon reached the ruins of a village that was now little more than a clutch of tumbledown buildings. The structures' roofs had collapsed long ago, and barely a trace of fences remained where gardens had once stood. Jonas went inside the old houses to see if there was anything worth taking, but it was clear the place had been thoroughly scavenged. Aside from a few broken pots, the buildings were empty. He investigated the well in the centre of the village, hoping to fill their water flasks, but found it dry. Just as well, because the bottom of the deep shaft was filled with bones. Whether they were human or animal, he didn't dare find out.

He returned to Halima to find her seated on the ground, using a shard of pottery to draw on the bare earth. Jonas drifted closer and saw that she'd inscribed a large triangle – the symbol of old

Havanthya. "We should move on," he said. "We're exposed here."

"In a moment," Halima replied. "Don't you know where we are?"

Jonas shook his head. "In whatever's left of some old human settlement. There are hundreds exactly the same across Anoros."

"Not like this one," said Halima. "We're in Arndal, where Thom was born."

"Really?" said Jonas, casting a disappointed glance around. "You believe all those old stories? That Thom was the nephew of a blacksmith? The boy destined to be Master of the Kind?"

Halima frowned. "Of course. Without destiny and purpose, we're no better than animals."

"What's wrong with animals?" said Jonas. "They seem happy enough. A nice simple life."

"And that's what you want, is it? If Thom had had the same attitude, he never would have left Arndal. He'd have grown fat on his aunt's cherry pie, like his uncle Henry. His sword arm would have been good for nothing but hammering horseshoes. Malvale's Kind would have wiped out all of Havanthya. All because one boy wanted a *simple life*."

"Yes, all right," said Jonas. "You've made your point."

Halima kneeled face-down on the ground at the triangle's furthest point, then rose again. "Thom was the greatest of all the Masters, pure of heart, loved by all, unyielding in his sacrifice to the realm." She looked deep into Jonas's eyes. "Every age needs a hero, Slayer."

He watched her repeat the bowing motion several times, uttering words in Havanthyan. He recognised in her mumblings the names of Masters past and of Ajuro and Dalthek; he heard her ask for the guidance of their spirits now. The prayers were the same that the shamans in his own village had once uttered.

And look what happened to them.

Jonas hadn't been able to protect them. What made him think he could keep Halima safe?

He found himself looking east again to the shadowy presence of the Forbidden Lands. He waited until Halima had finished her chants, then spoke.

"I have to go with Seth," he said quietly.

Halima turned on him crossly. "No, you don't. You want to, but you don't *have* to."

Jonas clenched his jaw. "You don't get it. Thom was pure of heart, loved by all, unyielding in his sacrifice, right? Well, I'm none of those things. I'm not good. I'm not brave. People *fear* me. Sometimes, I fear *myself.* Until I can find out why I am this way, I'll never trust myself."

"Thom trusted you," said Halima. "He gave you his breastplate. He chose you."

Jonas rapped his knuckles on the armour. "And this is all that stops me killing everyone I meet. Unless I can control my death-song, I'll always be a danger. I'm sorry, Halima. I have to find out what happened. I need to understand myself."

"You controlled it well enough in your battle with Kykyra, and I'm sure the Reader can help you do even better. Please, Jonas, we're almost there. You can't trust that wyvern. You said it yourself."

But Jonas shook his head. "Go without me. I promise I'll be there as soon as I can. You'll be safe with your people until I return."

The girl stood up and angrily brushed her foot over the triangle, scuffing it away. "And what if I'm not? What if I die because your past is more important than the future of humanity?"

Jonas swallowed. "The two things are connected," he said, remembering the sangwar roots. "What Was and What Will Be flow side by side."

"Spare me your mumbo-jumbo," said Halima. "Just admit you're a coward. You're scared to fight alongside your own kind, just like Resala." She turned and stalked off.

"It isn't that at all," said Jonas. But he wasn't sure if Halima heard him. She was already ten paces away, hair flying, striding towards the distant forest.

Jonas knew he could go after her, but his feet refused.

"You made the right choice," said Seth. The wyvern was seated on the edge of the dry well now. "She's scared, but she'll forgive you. Humans are fickle creatures."

"I'm a human," said Jonas sadly. Halima didn't look back.

I've let her down.

"But you're much more as well," Seth said. "Come on, let me show you."

10

IN THE TEMPLE OF THE CREATOR

"Where are you taking me?" Lana asked her escorts again.

Once more, they didn't answer. They'd arrived at her dwellings after dark and asked her to accompany them on an urgent matter. Bart had counselled her not to go, but Lana wasn't afraid. She knew she had many enemies in Whitestone, but if they intended to assassinate her they'd go about it in a far more discreet way than sending the Order of the True to her front door in the dead of night.

They entered the Temple of the Creator by a side entrance. The main chambers of the temple appeared to be empty and their footsteps clacked across its stone floors. The temple's glorious vaulted ceiling displayed Lana's own work – a colossal carving of the Spawning, all worked in pinkish veined marble. In its centre she'd depicted the Creator himself as he drew upon the last of the old-Kind essence. By the chamber's flickering torchlight, the marble magically shifted and flowed as the Creator brought forth into the world the new-Kind species.

Lana's escorts took her up a side stairwell, then down a gallery towards a set of double doors at the far end. One of the servants rapped on them lightly. When the doors opened, on the other side was a yellow-eyed face Lana recognised – Kezia, Chair of the Council of Magic-Kind.

"You can leave us now," she said to the Order members. She waved her hand, and both simply evaporated into grey mist. In seconds, they were gone.

"An illusion," said Lana. "Clever."

The magic was actually quite rudimentary, but it suited Lana to make Kezia believe she was impressed.

"I wasn't sure you'd come if you knew who had summoned you," said Kezia, grinning through her wolf-like fangs.

You're quite right there . . .

Lana smiled. "Why ever not?"

The conjuror's fangs were just another illusion,

of course. Kezia was human, though her ability to wield magic technically made her magic-Kind. This was a low rank among the Kind, though considerably above the status of regular humans.

Knowing Malachai's hatred of humans, Lana had at first thought it very odd that he had allowed Kezia into the Order of the True, much less supported her to become Chair of the Council of Magic-Kind. But this was before she'd discovered that Kezia detested regular humans as much as the Arch Protector, if not more. Kezia worshipped Malachai in all things and, as was clear from her fangs, her yellow eyes and the wolf-pelts she wore, wished nothing more than to be properly new-Kind.

Kezia waved a hand. "Politics," she said. "It's no secret everyone is jostling for position at the moment. But some things are more important. Come, follow me."

She led the way to a suite of rooms Lana recognised. Malachai's office had a sprawling basking balcony and walls stacked with heavy tomes. Deeper into the set of rooms, Kezia pulled aside heavy drapes to reveal a bed. The Arch Protector lay on his back, a sheet pulled up to his chest.

Lana hadn't seen the Arch Protector since the day of the cave-in under Skin-Grave. She approached the bed slowly. A male human servant was cleaning the scales on the Arch-Protector's face and neck with a cloth; Malachai wasn't moving at all. His eyes were taped shut.

"Has there been no change in his condition?" she asked.

The servant shook her head. "We speak to him and carry out physiological tests twice a day. He doesn't respond."

Kezia whispered something in the servant's ear. He gathered the ewer of water and scurried out, leaving them alone.

"I've consulted with doctors from across the Four Kingdoms," Kezia said. "We are none the wiser as to why he doesn't wake."

"It was a serious injury. These things can take time," said Lana, leaning closer. Malachai's chest rose and fell slowly.

"Yes, but unfortunately we don't have time," said Kezia. "Without Malachai, the Order of the True is leaderless. Our enemies sense weakness and are certain to take advantage."

Our enemies? Lana was sure that Kezia meant humans, though she was of the same species. But Lana knew Kezia would be all too happy to forget that. She'd thrown her lot in with the Kind long ago.

"So why am I here?" asked Lana. "I'm no doctor."

Kezia eyed the shadow creeping over the right side of Lana's body. "No, you are more," she said. "You are connected to the Netherplane. You know spells that even those on the Council wouldn't dare to cast. I want you to try to wake him."

"Wielding that sort of power is dangerous," said Lana. "What if I harm him further?"

"We are desperate," said Kezia. "I've tried myself, but our translations of the ancient runes must be faulty. Nothing seems to work. But your magic is different. And you are Malachai's disciple; you were with him when he was injured. You owe this to him."

An edge of ferocity had entered Kezia's voice. Lana understood this was an order, not a request. However, it suited Lana for her master to remain in his comatose state. While he lay motionless in this bed, his followers would show her loyalty. They'd continue to look to her for guidance. But all that would change if he awoke. If that should happen, Lana would instantly be demoted once more to his apprentice.

No, Malachai must remain like this. But politics still had to be practised in all things.

Lana knew she must at least appear to do as Kezia had asked.

"If you haven't succeeded, I'm not certain I will fare any better," Lana said humbly. "But for the Arch Protector, I will try," she added.

Kezia nodded and stood back. Lana approached the bed and placed her fingers at Malachai's temples, then let her shadow flicker over his skin. Her lips moved, and she mumbled the runic spells. She sensed the power to pull Malachai back from the threshold of the Netherplane, where his spirit wandered aimless and without memory. She knew that with the correct incantation on her lips, all she had to do was reach out to lead his soul back to the land of the living. But she forced the words down, purposely garbling them so the spell lost its shape. She made her shadows dance more fiercely, but this was only a show for Kezia, who watched her intently with her yellow wolf eyes.

The spell well and truly collapsed, Lana completed her performance by bracing herself against the bed as if spent. Then, after inspecting the Arch Protector tenderly, she backed away.

"I'm sorry," she said, feigning disappointment. "It didn't work."

Kezia's face hardened. "Very well," the magic-Kind said, her voice clipped. "Thank you for your time and *effort*."

The way she stressed the final word made Lana worry her performance had not been as convincing as she'd hoped.

When Kezia spun on her heels to leave the room, Lana was quick to follow.

The human servant had been waiting at the entrance of the suite. Kezia ordered him to keep her informed of any changes. Once back in the corridor, Kezia asked Lana if she could see her own way back to the street, and Lana was only too happy to part ways. She returned to the main hall, sparing a moment only to admire her ceiling carvings once more. High above her, the Creator stood atop a mountain, his arms spread. At his feet, the enchanted marble of the earth and sky swirled as one, giving shape to half-formed creatures – wolf and bear, lizard and snake, bird and beast. As she watched, the Creator turned his head towards her, as if noticing her presence. His arm extended and he beckoned her to come closer.

"Hello, Lana."

The voice made her jump. Even the images of the new-Kind in the carving high above seemed to snarl in surprise at the sudden arrival of another figure. This one was a real person of flesh and blood, who'd appeared from nowhere. Though he wore a robe, his beaked face announced him as a crow-Kind. Caught entirely off guard, Lana summoned a giant shadow-ox to her side. It pawed at the ground, head lowered to defend her with its horns.

The crow-Kind did not seemed perturbed by her shadow beast, though he did stop a few paces away. "Impressive," he said. "Shadow is the stable form of raw magic – the element from which all the others were made. Yet, despite it being stable, it often has a mind of its own. Shadow is something of a mirror, reflecting the state of the person that wields it. I sense defensiveness in your display . . ."

Lana let the great ox vanish. "Who are you?"

"We have met, briefly," the crow-Kind said. He drew back his hood, revealing his feathered head. His eyes were yellow, unblinking and amused. And she knew where she had seen them before – in Skin-Grave. After the collapse that had buried Malachai and destroyed the Tablets of the Creator. These were the eyes of the giant white old-Kind crow who had swooped in to let the boy and the rebel thief escape.

"You were there," she said. "In the catacombs."

"I was," said the Kind. "My name is Gael. I'm a Gatekeeper from the Netherplane. I was once one of many, but now I am the last. And you, Lana

Shadowscale, have grown rather powerful since we last met." He raised his eyes to the ceiling. "It seems," he continued, "that you have absorbed the runes you saw across the Tablets of the Creator. Now you are able into invoke them through your shadow. You're able to cast spells without having to speak them."

It was unnerving that he seemed to know so much about her. Lana wasn't sure what he wanted. "You've been spying on me?"

"Observing," said Gael. "To be frank, I haven't sensed such power since I first emerged from the Netherplane with the Creator to help Him fashion the gateways to the Many Worlds."

Could the crow-Kind really be so ancient? Or was this a trick of some sort? Perhaps Kezia had sent him to test her.

"I live to serve the Emperor," Lana said calmly. "My powers are his to command."

"Ah, I see your vast talents do not extend to lying convincingly," said Gael with a twinkle in his eye. "Does the witch Kezia know your true loyalties and intentions?"

From some anteroom came the sound of shuffling feet. Probably just a member of the Order at prayer. "You should be careful here," Lana told Gael. "You were implicated in the attack on the Arch Protector. One word from me, and you'll be arrested."

"Do you really think so?" The crow seemed amused at the idea. "Won't you hear my message first?"

Lana wanted to get out of this temple and hurry home, but how could she not be intrigued? "You have another minute," she said.

Gael nodded. "Then forgive me for being so blunt, but I believe you are destined to play a part in the Cleansing. Along with the boy called Jonas."

"Slayer?" said Lana.

"Grashkor is dead, and the boy is now free to follow his own path," said Gael. "You two must find another – a third – and walk the way forward together."

"I have no time for prophecies and destiny," Lana said. "I am here to restore my family's name."

"Only that?" asked Gael. "Is it only renown that you seek? The applause of crowds, the gleam of riches – that sort of thing?"

"I also crave peace," said Lana. "But to have peace, I must first have power."

"Peace comes from balance," said Gael. "You must share the burden. Find Jonas, and find the third of your company."

"I am stronger alone," said Lana.

"Lahara thought the same," said Gael. "And look where it got her."

"What do you know of my mother?" asked Lana.

"Everything." Gael pulled his hood up once more. "I am friendly with the Mothers of Fate," he said. "Lahara didn't accept her limitations and refused help when it was offered. The power of the Netherplane overwhelmed her, and it will do the same again to you if you're not careful."

"I am careful," she said. "I wield my magic with caution."

"You lie again, but only to yourself," said Gael. "Listen . . ." His voice became more earnest. "Raw magic is seductive, intoxicating; it makes you lose perspective. Once you lose perspective, you lose control." He reached into his cloak pocket and took out an object. "Take this." He threw it to her, and with a gust of shadow Lana stopped it in mid-air between them. Drawing it closer, she saw it was a white jewel, the size of a plum.

"What is it?"

"Your shadow-blessing is a gift from the Netherplane," said the crow-Kind, "but without constraint it will be a curse as well. This crystal will help you control it. It will let you fully separate the shadow from your body."

"I need no gifts from strangers," said Lana. The white stone could be absolutely anything. For all she knew, it could be simply a spying device.

"I offered that very stone to Lahara too, but she refused," said Gael. "She thought it would diminish her powers. Don't make the same mistake as your mother. Sooner or later the shadow will threaten to overwhelm you, as it did her. The magic in this stone will ground you. It will keep you from being swept away. It will help you remember yourself."

A cough sounded nearby, making Lana spin around in time to see a priest shamble from the far side of the chamber. He was trailed by two monkish students. Soon, it would be time for dawn prayers. Lana turned back to the crow-Kind, but he was already gone.

His white jewel remained, still floating before her on a cushion of shadow.

Lana, with a thrill of trepidation, plucked it from the air.

It had been a night of surprises indeed.

11

THE FORBIDDEN LANDS

"You made the right choice," said Seth. "That human girl was a distraction."

They were heading east, and Jonas had to squint against the rising sun. Seth would fly sorties ahead, landing and then waiting for Jonas to catch up, as if he was in a hurry to reach their destination. It reminded Jonas of the games of tag they'd played when he was a child, when life was much simpler. *Nothing* was simple now, least of all his relationship with Seth. Halima had warned him not to trust the wyvern, but she needn't have bothered.

Jonas no longer trusted Seth at all.

Every time the wyvern looked at him, Jonas sensed greediness in his eyes. Perhaps even cunning, like he was trying and failing to suppress his eagerness.

Yet Jonas knew he needed him.

"She only wants what's best for her people," he said.

"She's been brainwashed by that Reader woman," said Seth. "Don't fall for it. Humans are no better than Kind. Once they have power, they'll slaughter their enemies just as brutally as their enemies once slaughtered them. Just look at how they laid waste to the old-Kind. This is the story of the world: a tale of predator and prey."

Which are you? Jonas wanted to ask. *And which am I?*

"How much further?"

Jonas was in a hurry too. If the answers to what happened to his tribe were in the Forbidden Lands, he had to find them. Perhaps he could speak properly to the ghosts of his people. To Fran. He couldn't trust Seth any more, so they alone could tell him what had happened the day death visited them.

"We're here, actually," said Seth.

Ahead, a drystone wall had appeared out of the haze. Seth flew over to perch on top of it. It was only waist high, and Jonas wondered what it was meant for. Looking closer, he saw the stones were etched with spidery runic symbols. Seth took a deep breath and sighed contentedly, as if the air somehow tasted fresher here. "Climb over."

Jonas hoisted himself on top of the wall and dropped to the other side. He felt the change instantly. The sun vanished behind clouds and the air cooled. His arms puckered in gooseflesh, and when he looked down, he gave a yelp. He could see through his clothes and skin to the ground beneath.

"Calm down," said Seth. "This place recognises its own. You're part ghost-Kind, just like me." He tapped his chest. "Look again."

Jonas again looked down at his ethereal body. It was an unnerving sensation. In his chest, where his heart should be, there was a ball of red light with a fleck of green in its centre. "What is that?" he asked.

Seth's chest was marked too, but the colours were in reverse – a green heart with a glimmer of crimson at its core. "Our shared life force," said the wyvern. "Here you see how bonded we truly are. Now come."

Seth led him deeper into the Forbidden Lands. The ground at Jonas's feet was like fine sand, soft and yielding. The strangest thing was that his feet left no prints; whatever indentations he made somehow filled as soon as he lifted his soles. With Seth at his side, they soon reached a forest – or rather, a forest appeared in front of them. One moment the way ahead had looked like an empty expanse, and the next Jonas was faced with a horizon of trees. Leafless, their branches clawed at the sky.

"We have to go in there?" asked Jonas. When he turned to his companion, Jonas saw he was gone.

"So much for brothers . . ." he muttered. His voice sounded oddly flat, as though it was dropping to the ground as soon as it left his lips. He tried to push out the fear worming its way into his heart.

He considered turning back, but that would be the cowardly option. He'd come this far. If he gave up his quest for truth now, how could he ever claim to be serious in wanting to know the secrets of his past?

He drew a sword from his back as he approached the treeline. Whatever dangers lay ahead, he'd meet them with steel.

It was even gloomier among the trees. After a while, he noticed that some of the trunks he passed glistened with dark sap. When he touched it with his fingers, they came away stained crimson. He'd been spattered with the gore of his enemies enough times to know what it was.

The trees were *bleeding*.

As the realisation entered his head, so did the memories: the scent of blood throughout the camp followed by the screams of his people. He tried to shake his head free of the awful sounds, but the screams seemed to linger, not in his thoughts, but howling through the branches, as if memories were somehow made real in this sinister place.

"*Jonas.*"

The voice calling to him was a child's. A girl's.

Fran.

"Jonas, help us!"

"Fran!" he called back, setting out in the direction of the sound. He didn't know if it was the powerful memory again or if she was really here. Maybe in this place there was no difference. "Fran, I'm coming!"

He began to run through the trees. As he did, he heard another set of footfalls, faster than his own, and coming from behind. As he spun around, he saw a bear loping between the trees. Its huge muzzle was lowered and its teeth were bared. When the creature was ten paces away, it pounced. Its forepaws were poised like daggers and just as sharp.

Jonas stepped aside and made a cut with his sword, slicing up through the bear's belly. The blade met barely any resistance before the attacker exploded into dust. Jonas watched the fine sediment settle across the ground.

A hallucination?

The screams of his tribe that filtered through the trees had intensified, but it was almost impossible to say where they were coming from.

Why hadn't his death-song warned him of the approaching danger? Was it silenced here in the Forbidden Lands? Perhaps that was why Seth had brought him. What if Seth wanted him vulnerable?

A branch stirred in his peripheral vision, and with a crack of wings a bird launched itself towards him. It was an immense eagle, its wingspan at least as great as a man's height. Its hooked beak glinted as it dived between the trunks, its yellow eyes fixed upon him. Jonas ducked to let it pass, but it wheeled and came at him again, this time talons first. He impaled it against a tree with the tip of his sword and watched it crumble to dust just like the bear.

Were these ghosts or merely figments of his imagination?

The screams still filled his ears, rending his heart

and mind. He wanted them to stop.

"Please," he said. "I can't find you."

He turned on the spot, wary of more attackers, but there were none. He began to walk, trying to pick the source of the screams from the strangeness of the woods. For the first time he could remember, he was truly afraid. He had no idea from which direction he'd entered the pathless forest, or how to get out. What if this place was a trap? A sort of hell where one was plagued by the torments of the past? He might be destined to fight shadows and hear the death-cries of his people until the day he died, or until he went mad and dashed his brains out against a tree to end his torment.

As he walked, hand tight on the hilt of his sword, he felt another presence. This felt different to the bear or eagle. More . . . substantial. He smelled a creature's acrid breath, its heavy bulk.

Along with his sense of this stalking presence, Jonas's death-song had returned. This was a relief, though its vague visions weren't much comfort: his throat being savaged by teeth or his arm being ripped off as easily as soft bread pulled apart.

Then, through the trees, he saw a pair of red eyes, glowing like hot coals. He stood his ground and drew his second sword. The eyes grew as the animal advanced, taking shape from the gloom. Moonlight caught silvered hair, rippling over muscle. The ground trembled under the creature's footsteps. A giant wolf.

"I've been waiting for you," she said.

Though her mouth had not moved, Jonas was sure the voice came from the creature.

"What do you want?" he asked. Already he was assessing weak spots – the neck, the armpit, the eyes. It would be a fierce fight, but he trusted his death-song to protect him.

"I am Moonfear, granddaughter of Lunar, the old-Kind defeated by Thom. Seth has spoken of you at great length."

I bet he has, thought Jonas.

"Where is Seth?" he asked. "I'd quite like a word with him."

"Not far away," said Moonfear. "But this is a place where you must face your fears alone."

"I'm not afraid of you," lied Jonas.

Moonfear gave a hissing cackle. "You should be. I am the terror that lurks in your heart. The horror you dare not approach. The dread of your past, and what this means for your future. You cannot achieve your destiny unless you stare your fear in the face." As she spoke, her eyes burned hotter than ever.

"Look at it," she said. "Embrace it."

Jonas's death-song flared under her smouldering gaze. It showed the many deaths approaching him.

When she launched herself at him, he was ready.

12

THE END OF WAITING

Gael paced his chambers, high up in the keep of the Lost City.

The oscilloscope perched on the window ledge spun wildly whenever he neared it. Brief though his encounter with Lana had been, her shadow-magic had left its mark on him. And despite the toil of teleporting to the marble city and back again, he felt energised. The power thrumming through him reminded him of the Netherplane, where he was born. Where magic always sang in the air.

Feeling these potent energies again made him decide something. When this current business was finished, Gael would return to the Netherplane to live out his final days in those currents of endless magic. He'd toyed with the idea before, but this time he really meant it.

But first, he must see through these events with Jonas the Slayer, Lana Shadowscale and the mysterious Reader.

For centuries, he'd been a detached observer of the affairs of humans and Kind, but this time it felt different. This time he sensed how deeply the unfurling events *mattered*.

Yes, this time he would finally stop watching and play a role of his own.

"And it will be the last thing I'll do in this world," Gael whispered.

"Are you all right?" asked the Reader.

He looked up, surprised to see her standing in the open doorway.

"You could have knocked," he replied.

"I did," she said. "You didn't notice. Hence my question."

"Ah, right." He busied himself with his instruments. "Must be my hearing. When you've lived for almost a thousand years, things start to . . ." – he tapped an anemometer that had stalled – ". . . malfunction."

He'd decided not to tell the Reader about his visit to Whitestone or the meeting with Lana Shadowscale. As a member of the Order of the True,

Lana was technically an enemy of the rebels, and he was fairly certain the Reader would disapprove.

"You forget I can look into your thoughts," she said with a wry smile. "I can sense the hearts of people. You're keeping something from me."

"Am I?" said Gael blithely.

The Reader narrowed her eyes. "Something about . . . Whitestone. You disappeared earlier, so my assumption is you travelled there. Consorting with our foes, I expect."

"Urgh," said Gael. "Remind me never to make friends with a psychic again."

He told her what he had done, and she didn't seem surprised or cross so much as doubtful.

"You trust her?" she said.

"I want to," said Gael.

"And what if she tracks your magical energy here? She could lead the imperial forces right to us."

"I don't think she's that way inclined," said Gael. "In fact, I'm more sure than ever that she could be our ally – the third figure destined to usher in the Cleansing."

The Reader snorted impatiently. "Not this again."

"Three saviours to rebalance the world," said Gael. "Lana, the ruler; Jonas, the warrior; and you, the witch. It was always so in the days of Havanthya.

The triangle of peace."

"I wish I had your confidence," said the Reader. "But I prefer action to hope. Are you ready to help Alia recruit Aephos to our cause?"

Gael looked up innocently. "Oh, is she still struggling?"

The Reader cocked her head and gave him a withering stare. "It would make it easier if she had the red jewel you're hiding."

Gael tried to remain unflustered, but he guessed his prickled feathers betrayed him. "Is there *anything* you don't know?"

"That will be my secret," said the Reader with another smile. "But seriously, Gael. I know you don't think she's the chosen one, but at least let her try. What harm can come of it?"

"Very well," said Gael. "After lunch. Now, if you wouldn't mind, I need to rest."

"As you wish," said the Reader, leaving with a bow.

Gael listened to her footsteps descend the stairs, then went to the table where he'd left the volume of the *Chronicles*. He had no intention of resting, but the Reader probably knew that as well as she seemed to know everything else.

He found his bookmark and opened the tome up again to the place he'd reached in the story of Seth and the twin dragons.

He had no problem giving the red jewel to Alia, but Gael knew it would be pointless. Even if she could talk to the great phoenix, she'd never be able to control the old-Kind. The *Chronicles* made clear that only a Master of the Kind could win the trust of a creature like that. The jewel itself was a tool only a Master's hand could wield.

Gael turned the parchment page and ran a finger along the faded text. Thom and Helenya had tracked down Krimios, the red-scaled dragon, and begun searching for his green-scaled twin, Vedrios.

The adventures of Thom and Helenya often took unexpected turns, but this was a strange tale even for them. The twin dragon hatchlings shared a life force, and their connection acted as a sort of living compass, one always pointing to the other.

Both carried an aura of energy at their centre: Krimios's aura was red with a green centre. When he faced in the direction of his green-scaled twin, the green orb at his centre glowed more brightly. When Thom and Helenya discovered that the corrupt human boy Seth had cursed the gentle green-scaled Vedrios with an evil spell, they acted quickly to save him. Eventually, with the help of Aephos and Fernwing, Thom had been able to bring Vedrios to safety.

But the tale of the twin dragons didn't end there. Thom encountered the pair several times throughout his celebrated life as Master of the Kind, though the story in the Chronicles that caught Gael's attention took place decades after the days of Thom.

He read with an increasing sense of dread about the brother dragons' final tale, in which they were both cursed into violence and fury once again. This time there was no true Master of the Kind to protect them, and the saga ended with Krimios the red-scaled dragon killed by desperate humans. Though Vedrios survived the attack, he swore revenge for his twin's death.

The tale was simple enough, as these things went, yet Gael found that his throat had gone dry. Twin dragons, one bent on slaughter because of a curse, and an ending that left several questions hanging. It was a tale that echoed through the ages, and he cursed himself for not hearing those echoes until now. If his suspicions were correct, it could unravel everything.

If his fears were well founded, Jonas was in terrible danger.

Gael closed the book and fished out his purple jewel. He had to find the boy. He had to warn him.

He lifted the jewel, ready to create a portal, when from far off came a thudding *whump*. His instruments flew from the sill and crashed across the floor, and for a second Gael felt weak at the knees. He knew a magical shockwave when he felt one, and he rushed to the window. Below, everyone had stopped what they were doing. The soldiers stationed across the battlements all pointed to the south, where the sky rippled like a huge stone had been dropped into a pool.

Something had happened to the forcefield surrounding the Lost City.

Gael quickly scurried to his case and found his monocular with the rockglass lens in place. He returned to the window and placed it to his eye. He scanned the forest, where smoke rose from the remains of the arch of Skurich.

"By the Creator . . ." he mumbled.

Swarms of insect-Kind soldiers flew in from the horizon. They carried scimitars and wore redsteel armour emblazoned with strange symbols. Not an imperial force, but some other mercenary band. An incredibly large and well-armed one. Hundreds of warriors launched themselves from the trees and Gael heard their buzzing advance, like the coming of a hurricane. On the ground, roach-Kind shuffled in a rapid formation of armoured shells and clacking, steel-tipped mandibles.

The humans who'd been tending the fields fled the horde for the safety of the city's walls.

A trumpet call went up from the battlements – three blasts in quick succession. Soldiers scurried to their battle stations around the city's ballistas and catapults while archers filed into position. Human troops marched in their ranks through the streets below, urging people into their houses. Orders were barked among the cries of panic.

Gael felt a trickle of guilt. Had the Reader been correct? Had he somehow led the Kind's armies right here to the human stronghold? Worse, had Lana Shadowscale betrayed him?

Doubts flooded his mind. Perhaps he'd kidded himself that he was in control, moving everything like the pieces in a board game.

All the while, the enemy approached – relentless and never-ending. He saw all his hopes coming undone.

Unless some saviour reached them, the Lost City would again fall to ruin and slaughter.

13

THE MOTHERS OF FATE

*L*ana used her shadow-magic to surround herself with a cloak of invisibility.

This didn't dampen the soft shuffle of her feet, but the streets of Whitestone were mercifully empty at this time of night. She hoped Jun would have no reason to check her chamber back at the house – her human friend certainly would not approve of this excursion into the darkness. Indeed, Lana herself could hardly say why she was risking such a trip the day before the vote for the new emperor. Anything going wrong at this stage could jeopardise her plans.

Yet she'd felt compelled to venture outside. In her pocket, she cupped the white jewel Gael had given her. The things the old crow had told her, particularly about her mother, raised questions she couldn't get out of her mind.

Did Lana truly have a role to play in the Cleansing? If Gael wouldn't tell her, she knew others who might.

Her mother, Lahara, had once belonged to the Mothers of Fate. This order had been one of the three pillars of rule supporting the Emperor, along with his court and the Order of the True. Paranoid about their influence and unsure of the Mothers' loyalties, Malachai himself had successfully lobbied to disband them. Officially, the Mothers no longer existed, but Lana knew that wasn't quite true. A small group remained in the network of caves beneath Whitestone, practising their vision-magic as they had done for hundreds of years. As long as they didn't interfere in imperial affairs, Malachai tolerated them. Lana wasn't sure how they'd receive a visitor, but she had to try.

The entrance to the tunnels was beneath one of the city walls, sealed by an iron gate. The wall here was lined with preening ravens, and the gate itself guarded by two soldiers belonging to the Emperor's Own. Lana's heart sank at the sight of the guards – she'd hoped not to encounter this sort of security. However, as she approached, one of the ravens perched above let out three raucous squawks, almost as if it had detected her presence. A guard took hold of a winch handle. In a few turns, the gate creaked open.

"The Mothers are expecting you," said the other guard.

Lana didn't know whether – or *how* – they could see her, but she cast aside her invisibility and hurried across the threshold. Within was pitch black, though this absolute darkness lasted only for a moment. Torches flared into life along the earthen walls as Lana made her way down the damp corridor. Legend had it that these tunnels had been dug by Quargos, an old-Kind who resembled a giant beetle. From the irregular scars in the walls and ceiling, it wasn't hard to imagine some giant creature excavating them. They reminded her of the mines of the Burrows back home, and she felt a pang of longing for that simpler life before fate brought her to this city.

Even as this homesickness struck her, the magic permeating the tunnels was a comfort. All around her, she sensed the composition of the earth and stone, and she knew she could bend it to her will.

There were plenty of forks and branches in the tunnels. It would have been an impossible maze to navigate in darkness, but Lana's path was guided by the torches, which illuminated only a single way ahead. She put her trust in their magical light. If the Mothers knew of her visit, they must approve of her arrival here.

And yet her fear didn't entirely release its grip on her heart, and she kept a close watch on the shadows beyond the reach of the torchlight. They seemed to dance on the verge of forming unnatural shapes: people, landscapes, images of the past. Until – after taking more turns through the warren of tunnels that she could even count – she *did* see a figure ahead of her. It matched its pace to hers to remain constantly at the edge of her vision. Lana thought about calling out for it to wait, but somehow she knew it wouldn't. It led her onwards.

Such a shadowy figure might seem sinister, but instead there was comfort in its presence. More than that, there was something *familiar* about it. Something in the shadow-magic of the air reminded Lana of her mother. After all, hadn't Lahara ventured through Quargos's passageways many times in her service to the Mothers of Fate? It was possible something of her spirit might linger here.

After she had walked for what felt like half the night, the tunnel finally widened and Lana found herself on the edge of a vast cavern. Torches at the perimeter threw light upwards to illuminate rough walls of stone. Algae, plants and patches of moss grew across the rock, dripping and glistening with water. In places, seams of green metal ore gleamed. Fifty metres up, the space was open to the night sky. The full moon hung above like a newly minted coin.

In the centre of the cavern, lying upon five biers hewn from solid rock, Lana found the Mothers of Fate. They were new-Kind of different species, but all wore the same plain dark robes. Lana had heard that the Mothers disavowed all material goods, living in isolation from the world, but it was still shocking to find them here, as still and lifeless as reclining statues on the lids of sarcophagi. She understood that this was where they meditated and had their visions.

Lana approached the Mothers carefully. As she neared them, she felt the presence of the natural elements: air, fire, water, clay, stone and metal. The only missing elements were shadow and ghost, though her uncle Bart would have argued these didn't count since ghost had no physical matter and shadow was the pure magic from which all the other elements were made.

"Greetings, daughter of Lahara," intoned five voices as one.

From the biers, one of the Mothers rose: a bird-Kind with the feathered head of an owl.

"Hello," said Lana, nervously. "I've come to—"

"We know why you are here," said the owl-Kind. "Follow."

The owl-Kind left the other Mothers and made her way towards one side of the cave. After a brief hesitation, Lana followed. Despite the woman's eerie tone, she wasn't afraid. If they'd been expecting her, there must be a good reason. The Mother led her through a roughly carved archway to a small, circular antechamber about three metres across, the ceiling of which barely cleared her head. Within, Lana saw deep scratches had been scarred on the earthen walls. She guessed these had been made with new-Kind claws. They formed the shape of a cloaked figure wearing a robe covered in spirals.

The Creator . . .

"Did my mother do this?" she asked. Her sense of her mother was even stronger here than it had been in the tunnels.

"These are Lahara's drawings," confirmed the owl-Kind.

Lana reached out to touch the wall, letting her

own fingers move in the patterns her mother had created years before. As she did, the figure's clothing rippled in response. Magic flowed from the Creator's image into her skin, and vice versa.

"Your shadows are powerful," said her guide. "Lahara was also able to see into the Netherplane, but not as well as you."

"That's not why I've come here," Lana said, because looking at her mother's mad scrawl, she knew what she had to do. She'd come to the Mothers for answers, but in her heart, she knew they didn't have them. Indeed, the answers she sought weren't to be found in this world.

Lana knew her mother had used incantations and other rituals to initiate her visions, but the time for enigmatic dreams was past. She needed to see more directly and more deeply.

She had to open a portal to the Netherplane itself.

When Lana slid the white jewel Gael had given her from her pocket, the owl-Kind's eyes widened.

"Have care where you venture, daughter of Lahara. The Netherplane is a dangerous place for the living."

Lana knew the Mother was right to warn her, but she also felt the power of the jewel throbbing in her palm. Gael said it would ground her, and that's exactly how Lana intended to use it. It would be an anchor to root her body in the world of the here and now. Her shadow would make the dangerous journey to the Netherplane while her physical body remained.

Lana had absorbed the portal-opening spell from the Tablets of the Creator, and she invoked it now. Runes flickered across the shadow-blessed side of her body, and on the wall ahead an oval of light formed, with white fire at its edges. Power surged across her skin, drawn to the jewel clutched in her hand.

She watched the stone glow, and then something incredible happened. The shadow that had always flickered across the right side of her body lifted from her hand – or rather, a hand *made of shadow* separated itself from her living flesh. She took a step forward, but it wasn't *her* foot that moved, it was the shadow's. When she turned around, she found herself staring at her own face. It was completely motionless, with eyes vacant like a living statue. But the oddest thing – almost uncanny – was the lack of shadow on the right side of her figure. Without it, Lana looked just like a normal lizard-Kind, albeit one frozen in time.

She gazed down at the form her mind inhabited,

one made entirely from shadow.

The owl-Kind had backed off, as if afraid.

But Lana was not. Though she had become two, she instinctively knew that as long as the white jewel remained in her hand, she'd find her way home.

Without any more delay, she stepped through the portal. For a moment, she stood in a world of pure light, but a scene slowly took shape around her. She was on a mountaintop amidst a range of jagged peaks that spread for miles to the horizon. She'd barely found her footing when the mountains melted and collapsed around her to become rolling waves in a gigantic pitching ocean. Her stomach rose nauseatingly into her throat as she slid into a trough of water. White breakers consumed her senses as they swallowed her. She raised her arms against the crushing weight of water, but just at the moment of her demise, she was on solid ground again. She stood in a tunnel carved with spirals. Skulls were embedded in the walls, staring out of empty eye sockets. Their jaws were open in silent screams.

A figure marched towards her with robes swirling at his back and a gnarled staff in his hand. A human form with a shaven head and unkempt beard. His eyes seemed focused on something beyond her and

Lana moved aside to let him pass. As he did, she saw the same spirals stitched with bright thread in his clothing.

"Well, aren't you coming?" he said. "After all, you're nearly there."

This was the Creator himself, the same man she'd seen in her dreams. She followed him down the tunnel. And just as the tunnel under Whitestone led to a cave, so too did this one. The very same cave, unless she was mistaken, but from a time long, long ago.

Where in the world of flesh, the Mothers of Fate had their strange vision beds, here was a lake. Gathered around it were the colossal old-Kind she knew from the tales of yore. The dragon Fernwing, with his great scaled tail and eyes like embers. Quargos himself, mandibles clacking and his shell gleaming in the half-light. Sephron bathed in the water, with only her head and shimmering green spine arching from the surface. Naynuk, the shaggy-haired cyclops from the icy lands, sat cross-legged and patient. There were others that Lana didn't know. Old-Kind of every shape and skin, pressing forward in a throng.

The Creator stepped to the edge of the lake and lifted his arms, his lips moving in ancient spells. As he did, a portal opened over the lake and from it shot twisted beams of silver light. These searched the air and struck the old-Kind. At once the large Beasts crumbled into swirling masses of dust and shadow. There was no sound and no sign of pain among them. Lana knew they'd submitted themselves to the magic of the Netherplane willingly.

At the edge of the lake, the Creator's arms moved in wild shapes. The swirling remains of the Kind moved as though they were an extension of his grip. Then he thrust out both arms, fingers splayed, and from dozens of amorphous balls of energy, new shapes were fashioned. They were smaller creatures with scales and wings, fur and feathers, shells and skin, tails and horns, hooves and claws.

"The Spawning," muttered Lana. She was seeing the moment the new-Kind had been brought into being, wrought from the life force of the old Beasts.

With a mighty gasp, the Creator dropped to his knees. The metamorphoses had clearly drained him. Then his robes fluttered and flapped as if caught in a gale. He rose from the ground, sucked towards the portal above the lake before vanishing inside it. As it closed at his back, the vision faded.

Lana was alone in the cavern, the pool completely still.

"A sacrifice was needed for the Spawning to come to pass," a voice whispered from behind her. Lana spun around to see two figures. One was the Creator, the other . . . her mother.

"For the Cleansing, it is the same," the Creator continued.

Lahara bowed her head. "Then take me."

The Creator stepped into the light. Across his face, spiral tattoos shifted in a dizzying spectrum. "You are brave, Lahara, but it is not so simple. The sacrifice must have my blood too."

Another vision of the past, Lana understood.

The two figures approached one another and joined hands. They moved closer, falling into an embrace as they kissed.

Lana's blood ran cold as she took it in.

My mother and the Creator . . . a couple.

She turned and fled back down the long tunnel. When she reached the portal, she threw herself through it.

In a heartbeat, she'd crashed back into her flesh body and collapsed on to the ground in front of the owl-Kind Mother of Fate.

"Lana, daughter of Lahara." The Mother rested a hand on her head. "Are you hurt?"

But Lana couldn't answer. She couldn't turn away

from the image of the Creator scratched by Lahara into the chamber's rock walls. Lahara had always called him "The Father", but Lana assumed this was merely a term of reverence for the man many believed to be a god. But now she realised her mother's words were all too deliberate. His blood ran in her veins.

Lana was the Creator's daughter.

And – if she was to believe the visions inside the Netherplane – she was also destined to be his sacrifice.

14

WHAT WAS AND
WHAT WILL BE

M oonfear's teeth find his throat. In two shakes
of her massive jaws, his head is torn off in a fountain
of blood.

Jonas's death-song showed his end. As the wolf
reached him, he side-stepped, spun and sliced, but
his blade passed through the pale fur without a hint
of resistance.

"You cannot kill me in this place," said the Kind.
"Your blades are useless here."

Her raking claw rips open his guts . . .

He leapt backwards as the wolf's terrible claws
scythed the air.

Moonfear lowered her head and charged. Her
bony forehead caught him in the chest and hurled

him through the trees. He rolled across the forest floor, hitting his head against the base of a trunk. For a few seconds he saw stars. When the world returned, it wasn't the one Jonas been in a moment before. Suddenly he was back in his tribelands, watching his people flee in fear. He heard the shamans' chants as he had that terrible day, though now he understood their words. They were calling for a sacrifice to begin the Cleansing.

Jonas saw his mother look at him with fear contorting her features as she screamed in terror.

He shook his head free of the horrible sight, only to see Moonfear standing over him. Her eyes blazed, and drool spilled from her black lips.

"Embrace the truth," said the wolf-Kind. "You have turned away from it for too long."

"I . . . can't," he said.

Her claws sink into his neck . . .

Jonas rolled away as she lashed at him. The wolf's claws tore bark from the trunk, spattering gouts of tree-blood across the ground and over his armoured chest.

"Why do you run from this?" she snarled. "You want to know what happened, yet you don't dare look in the place those answers lie – your own heart."

"I don't know what that means!" said Jonas.

Yet at the same moment, the red glow over his heart swelled. Licks of flame emerged from edges of his breastplate. Jonas staggered backwards as his arms seemed to change. Red scales – ghostly and translucent – spread across his limbs. From his fingers, talons extended like curved daggers.

"What's happening?" he cried.

"You are seeing yourself for the first time," said Moonfear. She paced towards him. "Do not look away."

He sensed a presence at his back and wailed in panic as two giant leathery wings burst from either side of his body. Powerful wings ribbed with thick bones and threaded with a network of pink blood vessels. He felt the weight of them in the muscles of his back. The heft of their power.

Jonas flexed his taloned fingers, and sensed their lethal force. He knew how it would feel to tear and rip, sinking them into soft flesh, and it brought bile to his throat. As he looked around, his focus sharpened and his gaze penetrated further into the trees. His ears picked up new sounds: the creaking of distant branches; Moonfear's soft breath. He smelled her musky scent. All his senses were heightened, just like when he inhabited Seth's body in one of his dream visions.

"Finally," said Seth. "Welcome, brother."

The wyvern stepped out from behind Moonfear, touching the wolf's heaving flank. Moonfear backed away, fading into the shadows before vanishing altogether.

"What am I?" asked Jonas. And as he spoke, his voice sounded and tasted different. He realised that he had a ghostly snout extending from his face. It moved in time with his words.

"Your true name is Krimios," said Seth. "Your body was murdered, but your spirit was too strong to die. My true name is Vedrios. We are brothers in Kind."

Horrified, Jonas shook his head. "No, this isn't me," he said.

This had to be a trick: some sort of ghost-magic. Something from the Netherplane must have attached itself to his body.

"This is the real you," said Seth. "It has been there all along, hidden inside that pathetic shell of human flesh since the day the shamans summoned it. How can you doubt you have my twin's spirit inside you? His song of death has protected you from harm so many times. You must not fight it any more."

Jonas looked down at his body, now covered completely in red scales which became more real, and less ghostly, with every passing second.

"Behold yourself," said Seth. "Let that wretched human body go. Together we can take our revenge on the humans for killing my brother."

"No . . ." said Jonas. "I *am* human."

"You're so much more than that," said Seth, his eyes gleaming. "Havanthya must not be allowed to return. If the Reader and the human rebels gain power, they will wipe the Kind from the world altogether – just like they killed the old-Kind. Just like they killed *you*. The human, Seth, was the first to show us the true face of mankind when he put a curse on me. And yet we were still lulled into forgetting their capacity for cruelty and thirst for power. This mistake cost you your life. I took the name Seth so as never to forget the greedy wickedness of humanity."

"So you are an old-Kind?" said Jonas. "All along, you were my enemy?"

"Listen to me," said Seth. He stepped closer, his eyes full of yearning. "I loved you. I protected you. Our spirits have always been entwined, so when they slayed my brother's body, a part of me died too. I became half ghost, able to shift back and forth between solid and ghostly form."

"But I don't understand," said Jonas. "How did Krimios's spirit get *inside* me?"

"We were patient. *Very* patient. And then we were lucky," said Seth. "The shamans of your tribe needed help from their ancestors in their fight for survival against the insect-Kind, so they opened a portal to the Land of What Was. But instead of their ancestors, it was I who answered their call. I led your spirit into a newly born human body. From that day forth, we were bonded anew. I was your protector and guide. With my twin's spirit growing stronger inside you, you became a boy who could deliver the Cleansing itself. But a sacrifice was needed for you to become all that you could become."

Jonas felt sick. He guessed what was coming. He'd seen it, he realised, in visions before, without truly comprehending what it meant. What he'd *done.*

"When you were thirteen," Seth continued, "the shamans opened a portal to the Land of What Was once again. They thought the presence of the ghostly lands would increase your death-song and turn you into your true form."

My true form.

"Their efforts were successful, though not in the way they'd hoped," Seth continued.

Jonas felt hollowed out. Sickened. He wanted to deny it, to scream that Seth was a liar. But he knew it was no falsehood. The cat-Kind priestess had seen Krimios's form scattering Jonas's people. His own visions – the ones that had plagued him since that day – took on a new meaning. The terrified faces of his tribe as they fled. The way their very eyes had seemed to bore into him, haunted by horror. It seemed so real because it was. They'd been looking at *him*, transformed into Krimios by the shamans' ritual, while he cut them down with his claws. Driven by the death-song of the old-Kind, he'd slaughtered his tribe.

Jonas fell to his knees and buried his hands in the ashy ground. He felt the ghostly spectre of Krimios fade away, leaving him back in human form. Tears welled in his eyes.

"Why didn't you tell me before?" he whispered.

"You were not ready," said Seth gently. "They were a sacrifice, and a necessary one."

"They were my people," sobbed Jonas. "My friends. My family."

"They were *humans*," said Seth, almost snarling as if the word disgusted him. "The very same humans who would wipe our Kind from the face of the world or bend us to their will as slaves. They thought they could use magic from the Netherplane to fight their battles, but they were wrong."

There was truth to Seth's words. Even in the depths of his grief, Jonas could acknowledge it. The shamans had sought power, and it had cost them dearly. But the others – the children, his cousin . . .

"They were innocent," he said.

"The blood their ancestors spilled had to be repaid," said Seth coldly. "What's done is done. Take off that breastplate, brother. Only then can you truly assume your power. Unite your two natures and fully become Krimios. Help me fight those who would enslave our Kind again."

Jonas stared up at the ghost-wyvern. Seth's green heart was almost too bright to look at. "You mean kill them?"

"That golden armour you wear is the mark of the oppressor, the so-called 'Masters' of the Kind," Seth said. "They are the true killers. Kind have no master. We want only balance."

"No, you want revenge."

"The leaders of this world will not want it restored to true balance." Seth flapped his wings. "Some must pay. But once they have been dealt with, we will finally have peace again."

"You lied to me. You lied from the start."

"I saved your life more times than you can count," said Seth. "And Krimios's death-song kept you safe. If I had told you before, how would you have coped? You were just a boy. I protected you from the truth, because I loved you like a brother. Because you *are* my brother. "

"No – *he* is," said Jonas. "Everything that's happened is because of him, and you. I was just a pawn."

"You were *chosen*," said Seth. "Take off the armour and grasp your destiny."

"Why? It's a destiny I do not want. I did not choose it."

Seth stepped back, nodding slowly. "Then what, Jonas? Will you live your life as a fugitive? Feared by humans and Kind alike. Haunted by the visions of what you did, plagued for ever by the ghosts of your family. I'm offering you the chance to forget. To let go of the memories of your past."

Jonas found his hands moving towards the shoulder clasp of the breastplate. Was it really possible? Could he scrub his mind clean of the horror of what he had done?

Seth crouched beside him. "That's right, brother," he said. "Shrug off your wretchedness. Soothe your pain with an eternal song of death. Leave the boy called 'Jonas' and his crimes behind. Become Krimios."

His voice was like cool water on a scorching day. It promised contentment. And when Jonas looked into Seth's green eyes, there was only kindness there. Yes, he'd lied and manipulated him. But Jonas also couldn't simply forget all they'd been through together. The lonely years of wandering, with only the wyvern at his side. Joking by firelight, hunting for food, surviving when the odds were stacked against them.

And what a relief it would be to forget! No more screaming in his nightmares. No more guilt. Nothing at his back, and only the Land of What Will Be ahead. He released one clasp on the breastplate and reached for the other. A weight lifted across his shoulders and from his heart – a flood of light and joy. The sky above seemed to brighten.

"Feel it," said Seth, smiling. "Isn't it glorious?"

Jonas nodded, marvelling at the buds on the trees and the warmth of the sun on his skin. He wasn't sure exactly where he was, but at least he had his brother here with him. Then there was a movement, behind Seth, among the trees. Seth looked too. It was a small person, peering from the shadows.

"Fran?" said Jonas. His cousin gazed at him

intently, silently.

Seth drew closer and forced Jonas to look at him. "Ignore her, brother. Let's take off this heavy armour."

Jonas turned again to his cousin. She looked at him imploringly and shook her head.

"What is it, Fran?"

"They need you," said his cousin. Her voice was soft and nearly muted, as if the air between them was too thick for words.

"Who?" he asked.

"At the Lost City," she replied. "Halima is in trouble."

"Don't listen to her, brother," said Seth.

Jonas pushed his hands away and stepped towards the trees where Fran was sheltering. She backed away a little. "Resala has attacked," she said. "The humans will fall."

"Good!" said Seth. "The tyranny of Havanthya cannot be allowed to rise again. Let them fall! Let them die! Let them all die!"

Fran vanished again, melting into the shadows. "Wait!" called Jonas, taking a few steps to follow.

Seth caught his arm. "Just a vision sent to deceive you, brother. She's the past you must escape from. A bad memory you can be free of for ever."

But Jonas heard the desperation in the wyvern's voice and saw the avaricious gleam in his eyes. He refastened his breastplate.

"I don't want to forget," he said. "I want to fight for my people."

Seth howled and launched himself into the air in fury. When he landed again, he growled at Jonas furiously.

"You could *die*. Do you understand that?"

Jonas hitched his chin. "I'm not afraid."

"A mistake, but so be it, boy," said Seth. "The Lost City is far away. The Kind will breach the walls soon and the streets will be a slaughterhouse by the time you reach them."

Jonas paused. Seth was right, of course. If only Gael were here, able to transport him.

He felt his chest swell under the breastplate as his eyes fell on the large pawprints on the forest floor.

Perhaps there was another way.

15

THE IMPERIAL VOTE

*T*he day of the imperial vote had arrived, and despite an outward show of celebration, the air was thick with tension.

Lana took her seat upon a stone throne in the central basking courtyard of the Marble Palace.

Her throne was one of nine arranged in a circle. These splendid seats were meant for the Imperial Candidates, who were also the very same electors who would cast their ballots for the next emperor. Lana was here to represent Malachai and the Order of the True. So far only two of the other thrones were occupied. From one of them, Silash the Court Speaker surveyed the crowds with narrowed eyes and tongue flickering through his jagged teeth. The

Emperor had also been installed in his chair, though his bulk seemed to be flowing over the edges. He looked rather uncomfortable as servants attended with him with fans.

Lana cast her eyes across the crowd of spectators. In the background were the common Kind of Whitestone, with an area at the front reserved for nobles, military dignitaries and members of the Order of the True. There she saw Shahn and Uncle Bart seated, with Jun attending them.

Lana's eyes lingered on her little sister. She didn't know how to tell Shahn about the shocking revelation she'd had in the underground chambers of the Mothers of Fate, though she knew she must. As Lana studied Shahn's face she realised that she saw no resemblance to the lizard-Kind she'd once believed was their father.

Did that mean that Shahn too was a child of the Creator?

Their aunt, Florenz, sat a short distance from them, dressed in her finery. Kin, perhaps, but not family and certainly not someone Lana trusted in the slightest. Also watching from this section were Kezia and her associates from the Council of Magic-Kind.

The other candidates took their thrones. One was

a veiled elderly lady, representing the Mothers. Then came the lords and ladies of the Four Kingdoms' most powerful aristocratic families: two bird-Kind, two reptiles and a horned goat.

With all seated, silence fell over the courtyard.

Silash, in his dual role as Speaker and Imperial Candidate, rose. In his nasal tone, he spoke to all who had assembled.

"A sun is setting on the Four Kingdoms, but there will be no darkness, for another sun rises. The day has arrived on which we say farewell to our loving Emperor and choose a new leader to govern us. Let the voting begin, as is the custom, with the wisdom of he who is departing." Here, the lizard-Kind turned to the Emperor with a flourish.

He thinks flattery will win favour, thought Lana.

The Emperor gave a shallow bow in response. He took the voting stone from the arm of his throne, and made a show of casting his gaze among the eight candidates. Then he tossed it nonchalantly on to the stage in front of Lana. A gasp went up from a portion of the crowd, and Silash gripped the arms of his seat.

The Emperor's jowls shook as he addressed the courtyard. "Never before has a member of the Order of the True sat on the imperial throne," he said, "but Lana is of noble blood, Shadowscale blood, and her artistic eye and crafting skill will ensure beauty returns to the Four Kingdoms."

"She's just a girl!" roared a lone voice in the crowd, but it was joined by others. Lana heard the words "exile" and "crazy" uttered with disgust and incredulity.

"She may be young," said the Emperor when the cries had died down, "but she is powerful. Did she not prevent an attempt upon my life? I have made my choice. What say the Mothers of Fate?"

He turned to his left, where the representative of the Mothers sat. Without saying a word, she cast her stone alongside the Emperor's, at Lana's feet.

So far, so good.

It was Lana's turn next.

"I am humbled by the support of the Mothers of Fate and our Emperor."

She kept her eyes downcast as she dropped her stone in front of her own throne. Three out of nine votes already. Two more and she would be Empress of the Four Kingdoms.

She sensed the crowd's attention switch to Silash. Grumpily, he voted for himself and then pulled his robes close, as though shielding himself from a draught only he could feel. The five nobles remained.

Lana understood the dilemma they found themselves in. The way they cast their stones might well determine the good fortune of their families. Select the eventual winner, and they could expect largesse. Side with the loser, and they'd lose influence. The first to make their choice was a salamander-Kind, and it came as no shock to Lana that he tossed his stone in front of Silash. The hawk-Kind quickly did the same. Now the stakes were even, and Lana's anxiety grew. The momentum was with Silash and sure enough, the next vote also went his way, and suddenly she was trailing.

"A moment, please!" called a voice from the crowd. Everyone turned. Florenz was standing up. "Before we see the remaining ballots cast," she shouted, "I think you should all know what it is you are voting for. Lana is my niece, and as such she will enjoy the support of my wealth, my resources . . . and my armies."

"Your *armies*?" spat Silash. "Woman, you are a spice-trader, not a general."

"Is that so?" Florenz replied. She raised a hand to point at the sky. At first Lana saw nothing, but then, high up in the clouds, black spots appeared. A murmur rippled through the spectators. All eyes faced skywards as the dots grew. They were insect-

Kind – locusts – and on their backs they carried humans wearing armour the colour of blood. *Redsteel*. The riders brandished redsteel weapons too, and the combination of their howls and the buzz of the insect-Kind wings was deafening.

Panic set in as the warriors descended, with guards from the Emperor's Own stationing themselves around the stage and thrusting their spears skyward.

"What is the meaning of this?" rasped Silash. "This is treason!"

"No," said Florenz. "To the north, I have a great army of human tribesmen and insect-Kind. This army is loyal to me, and they would never raise a weapon against the rightful emperor. But know this – they will only raise their weapons *for* one empress. My niece, Lana Shadowscale."

Lana was caught out by the depths of her aunt's cunning. What a bold play for power, to use her military might to smooth Lana's path to the throne. Upon Lana's coronation, no doubt Florenz expected to pull her strings behind the scenes.

"Humans riding Kind? You expect us to accept this?" asked one of the other nobles. "And you arm our enemies with redsteel! It is sacrilege."

"These humans are the tribespeople of Morta," said Florenz. "They have sworn an oath against the rebels. They are loyal allies of Whitestone."

"Oaths made by human tongues are worthless," said Silash. "You expect us to believe you? I should have you arrested at once."

A few soldiers made a move towards Florenz, who held up a hand. "Then know this, before you act. At this very moment, my forces have the rebel stronghold besieged. They sit within our grasp, like soft fruits ready to be crushed. I have achieved what you have sought since the Spawning: the complete domination of your human enemies. Vote for my niece, and I will make it so. I will end the rebels for ever."

As the shock of her aunt's announcement wore off, Lana found herself impressed.

"I vote for Lana Shadowscale," said one of the two remaining nobles – the goat-Kind.

Silash stared at the final voter – a heron-Kind who swallowed nervously. "Very well," she said. "I choose Lana too." She threw her stone on the pile with the others.

Silash's eyes bulged with anger. Lana guessed money had changed hands prior to the vote – money thoroughly wasted. She stood up and lifted her chin. She no longer needed to play the shy and meek newcomer.

This is my moment.

She stared out at the crowd triumphantly.

"I thank the voting council for their support," she said. "For many generations my family lived in Whitestone, only to be banished by jealous rivals who feared our abilities. Now that we have returned, I mean to restore the Shadowscale name to its former glory and secure the Four Kingdoms for the safety and prosperity of all Kind!" The crowd roared its approval and Lana continued. "To that end, there are pressing matters that must be addressed. Since arriving here, I have seen too clearly how rife corruption has become. Families plot against one another, and ambitious courtiers have sought to undermine the Emperor himself. And so, as my first edict, I order the arrest of Kezia, Chair of the Council of Magic-Kind, for the enchantments she placed on our former Emperor." Gasps arose, and a commotion spread through the ranks of magic-Kind. Lana spoke over the noise. "Should the Arch Protector himself awake from his ailments, he too will be taken into custody for the same crime. These two vipers worked together to cloud the former Emperor's judgement and afflict his body. Until now, I dared not expose them for fear of retribution."

"You lie!" cried Kezia.

The bloated former Emperor shouted something as he tried to get to his feet, but no one was really paying attention to him any more.

"You will be interrogated," said Lana. "And you *will* confess."

The Emperor's Own – now the *Empress's* Own – moved towards Kezia's group. Her servants abandoned her side at once. But before the soldiers got close enough to reach her, Kezia split before their eyes, becoming five, then ten, then more versions of herself. The magic was primitive, but it sowed confusion, as the guards closed their hands on empty air.

"Bart, keep Shahn safe!" shouted Lana, fearful that the sorceress might attack.

Bart began to usher Shahn away, with Jun following.

The Empress's Own fanned out through the crowd, hunting the real Kezia. Lana let her worry fade. The sorceress couldn't hide for ever, and all the mercenaries and bounty hunters in the Four Kingdoms would soon be on the lookout for the disgraced magic-Kind.

As order was restored, attention again returned to Lana. She pointed to her aunt, beckoning her on to the stage. With servants holding the train of her gem-studded robes, Florenz joined Lana.

"Congratulations, niece," she muttered. "And glory to the Shadowscales."

Poor woman, thought Lana. *She thinks she's using me. Time to correct that.*

"My gratitude for your support, Aunt," said Lana, addressing herself to the crowd as much as to the woman before her. "With your armies you have shown the heights of what can be achieved. Peace between humans and Kind."

A slight frown creased Florenz's powdered brow and it pleased Lana to see her relative's discomfort.

"Thanks to you, we stand today with our foot on the throats of the rebels. Just a push will take their breath away." A few fists shot up in the crowd, along with a murmur of support. "We can crush an army, but can we crush a dream? We could kill ninety-nine of every hundred rebels, and the dream would live in the mind of each remaining one, more potent than ever. The embers of that fire would burn, ready to burst into flames again. Peace is not won by bloodshed, but by compromise and kindness. The bedrock of a great society is justice."

The crown had gone silent.

"What are you talking about?" whispered Florenz.

"The rebels must be cleansed!"

"The Cleansing is precisely what I speak of!" declared Lana. "For I have peered into the Netherplane to learn its true meaning. It does not mean the eradication of our so-called enemies, but a chance to start anew together in the spirit of peace. It is a means to cleanse society of our hatred and mistrust so we may live as one. We can return to the golden age of Havanthya, when humans and Kind lived in harmony. That was the Creator's goal when he brought about the Spawning. Equality between humans and Kind, not some new tyranny."

Florenz shook her head as anger clouded her features. "You think I'll stand for this? This *betrayal*? The rebels must be exterminated. And if you won't do it, I will!" She looked up. "Riders! Fly to the Lost City. Give the order to attack!"

The locusts began to rise, but Lana was ready. She thrust out a hand and channelled her shadow magic into leaping tendrils of fire. As each touched its target, the locusts and their riders evaporated into ash, which rained down on the stage. Shahn, still being ushered to the edge of the stage, looked scared and confused, but at her side Jun beamed with pride. Lana didn't think Jun would ever question Lana's loyalty to the human cause again.

"You underestimated me, Aunt," said Lana. She nodded to the guards. "Arrest this woman. Take her to the dungeon."

Florenz trembled with fury and fear as she was seized and dragged away. "You won't get away with this!" she screamed. "And you won't save the Lost City. The streets will run with human blood!"

The Head of the Military, a scorpion-Kind named Monash, approached and dropped to one knee. "What is your will, Empress?"

"Ready our soldiers," she replied. "We will meet my aunt's armies and deal with them."

Monash stood. "Our troops are mostly ground forces," he said. "If Florenz has airborne units, they will have an advantage."

"They will think that, but they will learn otherwise," said Lana grimly. "Because I will be going with you."

16

THE BATTLE OF STONEWIND VOLCANO

Jonas's hands clutched at Moonfear's silvered fur and he gripped the old-Kind's flanks with his knees.

They bounded through Arndal, eating up the distance with magical speed.

Staying balanced on the immense wolf was an act of will as well as physical strength. But Jonas knew it was more than brute strength that allowed him to ride the beast. A tenuous connection bound them: a sense of shared purpose, though Jonas knew this could be shattered at any moment. If that happened, he was sure the ferocious old-Kind would throw him off without another thought.

The old stories said Thom had been able to summon the loyal Kind to his cause. Perhaps this was a taste of that power.

They loped up a low rise, Moonfear's thundering paws throwing up earth with every stride. When they skidded to a halt at the top, her ribcage heaved over the bellows of her lungs.

From these heights, Jonas could see the rebel city below.

It was like a place from a dream. Sleek spires and colourful domed buildings all surrounded by a great white wall.

But if it was a dream, it was one on the brink of becoming a nightmare.

Resala's ground forces were already attacking the perimeter wall with ladders and siege towers. Fires blazed from several points inside the city, throwing up columns of choking black smoke. Above the battlements insect-Kind buzzed in deadly swarms.

We're too late, thought Jonas.

If Halima had made it to the city, she could well be dead already. And all because he'd gone off on his personal quest to the Forbidden Lands. Guilt twisted in his stomach. This was what Seth had wanted. To distract him, so the human rebels could be massacred behind his back. He cursed himself again. For years he'd given his ghost-twin the benefit of the doubt, never guessing at the depths of the wyvern's deception.

"Thank you, Moonfear," Jonas said to the old-Kind as he leapt from her back. He would have liked to have the great ghost wolf by his side in the fight ahead, but it was clear the journey had utterly exhausted her. He didn't want any harm to come to her. "You can return to the Forbidden Lands now."

The mighty wolf bowed to Jonas before bounding away.

"You took your time," said a voice.

Jonas spun around, hand on the hilt of the Sword of What Was. The figure suddenly at his side was Gael, the old crow-Kind he'd first met in the catacombs under Skin-Grave. The Gatekeeper must have crept to up him silently, or more likely materialised out of thin air. He wore a weary expression, with a few creases of desperation around his eyes.

"What are you doing here?" asked Jonas.

"Observing," said Gael. "Helping, perhaps. To be honest, I'm not sure I know any more."

Jonas drew his sword fully. "I need to get inside the walls," he said.

"Your blades will not be enough to defeat Resala's forces," said Gael. "Even with your death-song, there are too many."

"I have to try," said Jonas.

"Then your blood will spill with all the rest being spilled, and your name will be forgotten."

Jonas rounded on the crow-Kind in sudden rage. "Then *what*? Should I just *watch* it happen?"

The beaked old creature did not look perturbed. "You have a destiny," he said. "You must complete the Master's Road. Thom saw it, and so do I. Only then can you fulfil your role in the Cleansing."

"The Master's Road?"

"It was the ordeal all Masters once underwent."

Jonas scoffed. "I'm no Master. I'm *Slayer*."

"That was Krimios, not you," said Gael.

Jonas was startled. "You know?"

"I worked it out from the old texts," said Gael. "I'm sorry it took me so long. But I believe you can drive him out of you if you walk the Master's Road and succeed in bending four old-Kind to your will. You must trust in your goodness. Who *you* are, without Krimios inside you."

"I'm nothing without him," said Jonas. "He's the only reason I can fight. He's the only reason I've lived this long. He's controlled me, but protected me too."

"No. He's used you, as you have used him. You've come to depend on him, but that doesn't mean you *need* him. Now is the time to see what you can do when you tread that path alone. You must become a Master."

"And if I fail?"

Gael shrugged, as though to acknowledge this was a distinct possibility. "Then you tried. You have already taken on two old-Kind – slaying Grashkor and taming Moonfear, the Ghost Wolf of the Forest of Fear. If the phoenix Aephos submits herself to you, the title may be in your reach. Win over the great phoenix and the human rebels may yet survive." Gael reached under his cloak and took out a ruby half the size of his fist. Its facets scattered the sun's rays. "This gem will allow you to speak to the old-Kind."

Jonas stared at the glittering ruby for several long moments.

He had serious doubts about the Master's Road, but he knew the old crow-Kind was correct in saying he couldn't defeat Resala's armies single-handedly. The human rebels needed the strength of the phoenix to stand a chance.

Jonas took the gem from the Gatekeeper.

He didn't know if he could do this, but he would try.

"And where is this phoenix?"

"Stonewind Volcano," said Gael.

"Stonewind?" said Jonas. "That's a day's ride – if we had horses. On foot it will take us at least three." He pointed his sword at the city. "People are dying in the city *now*."

"Time is not on our side," agreed Gael. "But distance is no problem at all."

With a flourish of Gael's cloak, the world darkened and Jonas lost his bearings completely. In the next moment, Gael was coughing and they both stood on the black slopes of a looming mountain. The air smelled sulphurous and above them, bright orange lava oozed from a huge crater.

"You will find Aephos waiting up there," said Gael, recovering his breath. "Remember, the red jewel will allow you to speak to the phoenix. Good luck."

"You're not coming?" asked Jonas.

"I will wait for you here," said Gael. "The Master's Road must be walked alone."

There was no time to waste, and Jonas began to scramble up the mountainside. The rocks were warm beneath his hands, trembling faintly as the massive volcano stirred. Despite the lingering smoke and the steep climb, Jonas felt strong. Whether it was Gael's encouragement that helped him or the power of the golden breastplate, he wasn't sure. A crevasse blocked his path, but he leapt over with relative ease.

I see you, human, said a voice in his head. *Come higher if you dare. I'm waiting.*

"Aephos?" said Jonas. He squinted upwards, but the peak was swathed with ashy clouds. Was she up there, somewhere?

That is how I'm now known, said the voice. *But I have been called many other things over the centuries.* Epos. Flame Bird. The Fire that Is Reborn. *I have seen a hundred Masters. A hundred Pretenders too. I wonder, which are you?*

Jonas reached a near-vertical section, pocked with shallow handholds. He reached with his fingertips and found a grip, bracing his muscles to heave himself upwards.

You have some physical prowess, said the old-Kind in his head. *But it takes more than strength to be a Master. I see the corruption in your heart – a death-blessing. Just as with others before you, evil will eat away at you until there's nothing left. Like Thanner, who became violent and bloodthirsty through evil magic. Like Seth, who was seduced by the dark wizard Malvale.*

Jonas was sweating as he reached a ledge,

breathing hard. "Then help me," he said. "Let us join forces."

The volcano shook, dislodging small rocks and making Jonas stagger.

Help you? asked Aephos. *Why would I do that? I have seen the evil you humans do. Before the Spawning, we old-Kind were driven from our lands, our power almost destroyed for ever.*

Jonas climbed on, his muscles aching. "Not all humans are bad. Thom was your ally."

Thom was my Master long, long ago, said Aephos angrily. *I should not have been awoken again.*

"Thom gave me this breastplate," said Jonas. "He chose me. He thought I could bring balance to the world. That there was a chance for a new age where the Kind and humans can live in peace."

Again, the mountain quaked under his feet. *You lie!*

"No!" shouted Jonas. He slammed his fist against the golden breastplate. "Why do you think I have his armour?"

You are not worthy of it, boomed Aephos. *And I will prove that!*

Louder than the voice in his head, a very real screech sounded from above, making Jonas crouch and strain his neck. Through the smoke burst a colossal shape – a bird twenty times his size, with wings spread and trailing fire. Its hooked beak was scarred with battle wounds from ages past, and the dark orbs of its eyes reflected the fire from its feathers. Aephos swooped towards him, talons outstretched, each as long as a scythe but many times sharper.

Jonas's feet slipped from beneath him and he slid down the slope on his belly. For a moment he was engulfed in the Kind's shadow as she passed overhead. He found his balance again, sweat springing from every pore, and plunged into the smoky fog she left in her wake. All he knew was that he couldn't face such a creature here, on the exposed mountainside.

The little boy runs, came the Kind's voice. *But it's far too late for that.*

He felt her presence at his back and saw his end.

She picks him up, talons catching his ribs, and hoists him skywards. Blood spatters from his wounds as he cries out in pain. She carries him to the clouds, shaking his feeble body before tossing him aside like an unwanted scrap. His screams die as he falls and end abruptly as his body hits the ground.

Jonas turned to swing his sword. The blade

clanged helplessly off the Kind's talons, but the impact threw him headlong, scraping the skin from his arm as he slid to a halt. The phoenix's power was incredible – like nothing he'd ever felt.

I sense your death-blessing, boy, she said as she soared past. *You are nothing without it. I too am a creature of death. I have died and been reborn many times. But you will only die once.*

Jonas picked himself up again and staggered on. He saw a small ledge ahead and knew what he had to do. No blade could defeat the old-Kind, but he had to prove himself to her. To show her that he didn't rely on his death-song. Looking over his shoulder, he saw her wheel around. She was coming again, wings outstretched in a calm and deadly glide, her eyes fixed on him like a hawk attacking a fleeing rabbit. He pulled himself on to the raised ground and turned to face her. He sheathed his sword.

"I'm not afraid of you!" he roared.

Then you are a fool, she screeched in reply.

When she was just a split second away, her beak gaping, Jonas leapt upwards, twisting in the air. He came down hard on her back, rolling off one side. He threw out a hand and grabbed a fistful of feathers, hanging on for dear life. He sank another hand into the plumage as her body shook beneath him. Then she began to pump her wings, climbing higher.

Your tricks will be your death, said her voice through the red jewel. *The air is my element, but the fire is my true home. You soon will taste its flames.*

She rose, away from the volcano, tearing through shreds of thick smoke that made Jonas choke and blink away tears. "I need your help!" he yelled, trusting that the red jewel would let the phoenix hear his words over the howling wind. "Just as you once helped Thom."

For a moment, she stopped flapping, letting the thermals keep her aloft. Looking down, Jonas saw the kingdoms spread out in a vast patchwork around Stonewind, the rivers threading across the landscape of fields and plains and forest. From this great height, there was no sign of the war that threatened to tear these lands apart. From up here, the Four Kingdoms were beautiful indeed. No wonder Aephos was unmoved by the affairs of humans and Kind if this was her domain.

I have spent too long in this realm, said the phoenix. *Your troubles bore me. It is time to return to my rest in the heart of Stonewind.*

With that, she folded her wings, dipped her beak

and dived straight for the glowing crater below. Jonas could do nothing but cling on. To let go would mean certain death. But if the phoenix dived into the lava-filled crater, death awaited anyway. What had he been thinking? That he could somehow persuade the old-Kind to be his ally?

I should never have listened to Gael. He put his faith in the wrong person . . .

The air seared as they plummeted towards the volcano's boiling heart. At least it would be quick, he thought. Plunged into a pit of lava, the flesh would be stripped from his bones in a second or two. He closed his eyes against the heat, and against the inevitability of his death. Perhaps he would see Fran and the rest of his tribe again in the Land of What Was. He hoped they would forgive him.

Then he sensed a familiar presence. He saw a vision of himself from another's eyes and looked down to see a dim shape coming through the smoke.

"Seth?"

The ghost-wyvern had appeared below them, defiantly blocking the phoenix's path to the crater. Aephos swerved with an angry squawk, trying to bank away from the spitting pool of molten rock. But she'd left it too late. The crater's edge caught her trailing talons, and the mountainside reared to meet them. She went into a roll, and Jonas was hurled into the air. He did the only thing he could and threw himself clear, bracing his limbs for the impact. A mighty crunch and showering fragments of rock told him Aephos had hit the slope first, but a split second later he slammed down too. The impact knocked his breath from his lungs, but bounced him airborne. He tucked himself into a roll, doing his best to shield his head, and then slid to a halt.

The sky above was spinning, but slowly it came into focus. He sat up, marvelling to find himself in one piece. His arm dripped blood from a long gash above his elbow, but otherwise he was unhurt.

Finding his feet, he saw Aephos crumpled thirty paces downhill. Her head was covered in dust, with one wing wedged under her body and the other flapping weakly in the air. Jonas knew he might not get another chance and staggered towards her, his feet sliding in the loose scree. He drew his sword and placed it against the feathers of her throat with just enough pressure to keep her pinned.

"Submit to me, Aephos," he said.

Her glassy eye blinked. *You have bested me, Master,* she said. *I am yours to command.*

"He needed my help though," said Seth, landing on the other side of the Beast and giving his own wings a satisfied shake. "*We* bested you, old-timer."

A shudder went through the phoenix's feathers, and she reared up on her talons. "Vedrios," she said. "Is that you, youngling?"

Jonas didn't understand how Aephos knew Seth's true name, but he guessed some of the old-Kind could recognise each other.

Seth's mouth twisted in a sneer, but before he could speak, Gael also arrived. Looking surprisingly fresh, the old crow must have teleported to this altitude.

"Indeed it is," said the crow-Kind.

"You have betrayed your own Kind, Gatekeeper," said the ghost-wyvern. "You have sided with the humans."

"I only want peace, for Kind and non-Kind alike," said Gael.

"There can be no peace while they draw breath," said Seth. "You must see that. Humans will always seek to dominate and control the Kind."

Gael squinted at Seth. "Your ghostly form confused me before, but now it's so obvious you're just like the Vedrios of old. Arrogant, entitled and bitter at heart. You are wrong, young dragon. Humans are not evil."

"Thom killed my brother," spat Vedrios.

"He had to," said Gael. "Malvale's servant Seth cursed him. Vengeance is its own curse, you know. It's not too late to break free from your past."

For one moment, Vedrios seemed to consider Gael's words, but in the next he leapt into the air, attempting to flee.

He never made it.

With a single thrust of a fiery wing, Aephos struck the wyvern in mid-flight and pinned him to the ground.

"You forget that old-Kind fire can force a ghost-Kind into solid form," said Gael. "Handy, really."

"Let me go!" shouted Vedrios as he struggled against the weight of the phoenix's wing.

"It puzzles me," said Gael. "Of all the names you might have chosen, why 'Seth'?"

"Because he was my teacher," snarled the wyvern. For a moment, he ceased his struggling. "Not that I realised it at the time. He was the one who showed me that the Havanthyans were selfish tyrants. For a time I didn't believe it, but when my brother was killed, I saw he was right."

"Yet your brother wasn't killed, was he?" said Gael, nodding to Jonas. "He lives on."

"In that shell of soft human flesh," spat Vedrios.

"How can I be rid of him?" asked Jonas.

"You can't," said Vedrios, smiling. "While I live, Krimios's spirit lives too, inside you."

"That's not exactly true," said Gael, looking at Jonas. "This bond was sealed through a sacrifice, and so a sacrifice too can break it. An old-Kind must die in order to cleanse Krimios from your blood and Seth from your life." He turned from Jonas to stare the phoenix in the eye. "You know what must be done, Aephos?"

"Wait!" said Jonas. "You mean Aephos must die?" He didn't like the thought at all.

"She has died many times before," said Gael. "But first, you must go to the Lost City and help the rebels." He nodded towards Aephos, who lifted her wings.

This released Seth, who immediately flapped up into the sky.

"You'll lose," said the wyvern. "It's too late."

The phoenix let out a screech and snapped at Seth with her beak. But he flew higher, looking down at Jonas with hatred and disdain. "Last chance, brother. Choose your side carefully."

As Jonas looked up at the wyvern, he felt the power of Krimios in his heart beneath the golden breastplate. The sweet lure of the death-song was intoxicating, full of blood and triumph and glory.

But that was a fruit he had tasted many times before. A temptation he had fallen for again and again. Nothing good had ever come of it.

Jonas shook his head and stood alongside Gael. "I've made my choice," he said.

Seth scowled. "So be it."

His ghostly form vanished from the sky.

"It was a wise decision," said Gael. "Thom chose you for a reason. You are the last hope for the City."

"Can you teleport me there with you?" said Jonas.

"Not this time," the sorcerer said with a smile. "There are other troops I must rally." The crow-Kind gestured to Aephos, who extended a wing to the ground at Jonas's feet. "But I promise this will be nearly as quick."

Jonas swallowed at the sight of the colossal phoenix. He could feel the heat from her body, as though her blood was molten like the inside of the mountain at their feet. He placed an unsteady foot on her feathers, then clambered up her wing until he could sit astride her neck. He'd ridden many horses in his life, but this was very different. On horseback, he was in charge. But on Aephos, he felt like a passenger, completely at the mercy of the creature beneath him.

"Will she know where to . . ."

He turned to Gael, but the crow-Kind had already vanished.

In the next moment, the bulk of the phoenix shifted beneath him as she rose to her talons. He tightened his legs on her sides and gripped her feathers in his fists. She took two small steps and thrust out her wings. With a jolt, she launched them both into the air, and they left the slopes of Stonewind far below.

17

ASSAULT ON THE LOST CITY

*C*old air blasted over Jonas, but warmth rose from the old-Kind's dark feathers.

They flew through clouds that soaked Jonas's clothes to his skin, but he felt at one with the creature below him. He sensed how her determination married with his own. Was this the sort of bond with the old-Kind that Thom had known?

There was great peace and satisfaction in his bond with the great phoenix, but there was trepidation, too – they were flying swiftly towards an uncertain future.

When they finally burst through the clouds again, Jonas saw the grim reality facing the human rebels. Rays of sunlight fell across the landscape, shining down on the desperate battleground. The great city's outer walls were breached in many places and close to collapse in others. At their base lay piles of corpses of the insect-Kind who'd been killed in the assault. Yet more insect-Kind surged forward, dive-bombing the archers who remained on the battlements or carrying rocks to drop on the heads of the defenders.

But Jonas was relieved to see the inner walls remained standing. The city hadn't yet fallen, and most of the civilians would have retreated to its centre.

"Take us in!" he called to Aephos over the howling wind.

As you wish, replied the phoenix.

She angled her wings and set them on a gliding course. Jonas had no idea what the layout of the city was or where they might be able to land, but as they passed overhead he saw several promising courtyards. Pockets of hand-to-hand fighting were happening in the streets, with small bands of rebels facing human tribespeople armed with redsteel. Fires burned here and there. Jonas was about to bring them around to set down on a rooftop, when the death-song flashed in his brain.

A beetle-Kind crashes into his right side, and he

loses his grip. He falls, spinning and flailing, from the flame bird's back until his body hits the ruined walls below.

Jonas ducked just in time and the insect-Kind buzzed past. Another came in its wake, giving him time to draw his sword. A slicing blow caught its legs and its blood spilled into the empty air. The wounded assailant flew on, its path ragged and jerking, until it gave up and plummeted to its death. More aerial troops approached in formation, but Aephos saw them coming. She twisted and batted at them with her wing, easily scattering them. Jonas swiped at others with his sword, hacking at shells and wings. The creatures were relentless. Aephos snatched one in her talons and ripped it apart.

"Take us down!" cried Jonas. At just a push of his hands, the phoenix obeyed, descending in a swooping arc. On the walls, human rebels watched, and several archers brought their bows to bear skywards.

"We're on your side!" screamed Jonas.

They clearly didn't hear, or understand, because they released a volley of arrows anyway. Jonas sucked in his breath as one whistled past his ear. Others buried themselves in the phoenix's feathers, though they seemed to do little damage. Aephos descended until she was flying beneath the height of the wall, along the length of a wide cobbled promenade. Here, a dozen or so tribesfolk bore down on a cowering group of elderly rebels. Both groups began to scream at the sight of the phoenix. Resala's troops turned too late, just as Aephos slammed into them, talons first, bowling them over like skittles or crushing them under her bulk. A thump went through Jonas's body as they touched down. He slid from the phoenix's back in front of the astonished rebels.

"It's the ghost of Thom!" said an old man. "Only a Master of the Kind could control such a creature!"

"Get yourselves to safety!" Jonas shouted. "Help is coming!"

The people didn't need to be told twice, and they scattered into the surrounding buildings. Jonas laid a hand on Aephos's curved beak and looked into her glassy eyes. "Take to the skies. Defend the walls as best you can."

Aephos crouched and sprang up again. With a wave of blasted air that knocked over a cart, she took off and wheeled over the battlements.

Jonas spied a set of stairs leading up to the wall. He needed to find the Reader and work out a plan to defend the City.

That's if she's even still alive.

He drew both swords and scrambled for the vantage point. He was halfway up when he heard the sounds of clashing metal above. Human rebels were fighting hand to hand with Resala's tribesmen. Jonas leapt the remaining distance and came face to face with a stocky man in redsteel, his sword dripping with blood.

"It's you!" he cried. "Slayer!"

He must recognise me from the duel at Resala's camp.

The man brought a horn to his lips to raise the alarm, but Jonas was quicker. With a lunging slice, he detached the man's arm and the horn clattered to the ground. With the tribesman in shock, Jonas lowered his shoulder and charged. He pushed the man over the edge of the walls and didn't wait to watch him hit the ground far below.

A blow struck him on the back, knocking him to his knees and punching the air from his lungs. He turned, raising a sword instinctively, only to see a giant of a woman clutching a redsteel mace. She lifted it over her head to bash in his brains, but before she could strike, an arrow punched through the centre of her chest, the shaft quivering. The mace dropped, and blood gurgled over the woman's lips as she fell headlong. Jonas glanced over his shoulder to identify his saviour.

"Jonas?"

It was Halima, holding a bow with another arrow already against the string. Her face was smeared with soot and a trickle of blood had dried under her nose.

"You came back."

Jonas stood up, flexing his back. The mace must only have delivered a glancing blow.

"I told you I would," he said. He was relieved beyond words that the girl was still alive. "Where is the Reader?"

"I haven't seen her," said Halima. "But others say she and Alia are in the citadel in the middle of the city. We're losing, Jonas. There are too many foes." Her voice was almost breaking with grief and desperation.

"Gael has gone to find help," said Jonas.

"Whoever he's looking for better get here soon," said Halima, "or all they'll find will be bodies."

"Don't worry," said Jonas, "we have a secret weapon."

As he spoke, Aephos soared overhead. She carried a beetle-Kind in each talon, then hurled them into the walls and certain death.

Halima watched the phoenix, her lips parted in wonder.

"Meet Aephos," said Jonas.

As they tracked the old-Kind's progress, the great phoenix swooped low over the scarred battlefield outside the walls, scooping up the human tribesfolk. Jonas could hear their shouts and screams, even at this distance.

Resala's forces manoeuvred their siege artillery in an attempt to meet the threat, but Aephos was too deft and quick. Their volleys of arrows and stones fell short.

"We have to get to the citadel," said Jonas.

"Come with me," replied Halima.

Jonas ran after her, along the walls and into a guard tower. Spiral steps led downwards, back into the street, then they darted through narrow alleyways. Civilians peeked from the cracks of shutters and doorways.

They've nowhere else to run, thought Jonas. *And if Resala's forces triumph, they'll all be enslaved. Or worse.*

Soon he and Halima reached a large central keep – the citadel at the heart of the Lost City. Its studded wooden doors were guarded by soldiers wearing full armour and clutching pikes, which they lowered at

Jonas's approach. Halima, though tiny compared to the big men, marched up and spoke firmly.

"We must speak with the Reader. Tell her that Jonas has come."

The guards looked at one another, then one entered the keep by a smaller door set into the larger entrance. A few seconds later, there came three loud bangs, and the huge doors opened.

Stepping into the cool interior, they discovered the Reader and Alia, standing on either side of a table upon which was a model of the city. There were miniature markers to indicate troop movements. They looked up at the new arrivals.

"You have brought the phoenix," said the Reader gruffly. "I fear it won't be enough."

Alia wore leather armour, and a sheen of sweat shone on her skin, as though she'd recently come from the battle herself.

"Actually, Aephos brought *me*," said Jonas.

The Reader smiled grimly, with a glance at Alia. "Then Gael was right about you, after all. Thom has chosen his successor." She used a long wooden cane to point to three spots on the model plan. "Our enemies have entered the city in three places already. They are encircling us."

With a crash, one of the high windows imploded,

showering fragments of glass on to the floor below. From outside came shouts of alarm and the clash of metal.

"It won't be long until they take the inner walls," said Alia. "You should flee through the tunnels while you still can."

"No," said the Reader. "We make our stand here, for good or ill. If the rebels see me flee, they will not fight."

"They needn't know you have left," said Alia. "If you live, the cause lives too."

"There will be no cause if I take the cowardly path," replied the Reader.

The sounds of battle were growing closer. Jonas heard Aephos's distant screech, but even the old-Kind couldn't fight in more than one place at a time.

A bright lilac flash made everyone throw up their hands. As Jonas blinked, he saw three figures had appeared at the back of the room. One was Gael, and another was also familiar – a female lizard-Kind in white robes with one side of her body wreathed in shadow. She was accompanied by a woman in a drab servant's tunic.

The crow-Kind looked around at the fragments of glass and shards of masonry. "Thank goodness for that!" he said. "I was worried we might end up somewhere more hazardous."

Alerted by the commotion, the two guards from outside rushed in, brandishing their pikes. When their eyes fell on the lizard-Kind, they advanced.

"Fear not," said the Reader. "These are our allies . . . I think." She cocked her head.

"Actually, this is your new Empress," said Gael, coughing. "Roshni, meet Lana Shadowscale."

But the guards were still on high alert, their spear-tips raised.

"I hardly expect you to kneel," said Lana, "but I'd rather not have weapons pointed at me."

Now Jonas recalled that he'd seen her before, in the catacombs under Skin-Grave. She'd been with the Arch Protector Malachai just before he'd been crushed.

"Are you sure we can trust her?" he asked.

The human servant stepped forward. "My mistress is an ally to humans," she said. "And my oldest friend."

Alia spoke up defiantly, drawing her sword a few inches from its scabbard. "Forgive me if that isn't quite enough of an endorsement for me. Whitestone has never been good to our sort."

The Reader reached out a hand and stayed Alia's

arm. "The girl speaks the truth," she said. "I sense the goodness in this shadow-blessed Empress." The Reader nodded politely to the Empress. "Greetings, Lana Shadowscale. And welcome to you also, Gatekeeper. I hope you come with good news."

"My troops are on their way now," said Lana. "They should tip the battle in your favour."

"But why would you *help* us?" Alia asked.

Just as she asked this, another boom ripped through the building, and this time the roof itself shook, releasing a cloud of dust. Whatever Resala was firing into the city was finding its range.

"We are no longer safe here," said Alia. "I've tried to persuade—"

A beam dislodges, tumbling down. One end strikes his head. Tonnes of masonry fall in dust and chaos, obliterating their bodies.

"Move!" Jonas shouted.

A tremendous crack reverberated through the keep. Gael immediately lashed his cloak around Lana and her human servant and the trio vanished. Jonas leapt towards Halima, driving into her with a force that lifted her off her feet. Great shadows enveloped them, and there came a noise of grinding stone. They hit the floor, and he kept his body over hers, expecting at any moment to be buried alive.

When the crash and roar of rockfall finally ended, he shook off dust and fragments, coughing and wiping his eyes.

"Are you all right?" he asked Halima.

She looked up and nodded meekly. "I think so. What happened?"

Light poured through a gash in the citadel's roof, where the wooden beams were shattered and the stonework had collapsed. "Direct hit," muttered Jonas.

Through the choking clouds came Alia's voice. "No! No, please . . ."

Jonas stumbled in the direction of her sobs, fearing what he would find. She was keeling on the ground among the debris. Gael had apparently transported back, and he, Lana and her servant rushed from the other direction. A large section of jutting masonry, still carved with the shapes of leafy vines, lay on top of the Reader's chest. Her skin was very pale, with blood trickling from her lips as pain flared across her features. Jonas knew at once from the sheer size and weight of the stone trapping her that she wouldn't make it.

"We can get you out," said Alia, heaving vainly at an edge. She twisted to Gael. "Use your magic, crow," she said. "Help me, damn you!"

"Oh, Roshni . . ." said Gael. He shook his head as his eyes surveyed the damage. "Don't move. I'll think of something."

"It's too late for that," said the Reader weakly. "My time is run, old friend."

"Don't say that," said Gael, his eyes moist. "We can get you to the best doctors in the Four Kingdoms. They can fix you."

"You're too old to believe in miracles," croaked the Reader with a thin smile. "But you're not too old to believe in fate. You were right: Jonas *is* the Master."

"Don't talk," said the crow-Kind. He gently took her hand. "Save your energy, Roshni."

Alia was openly weeping, stroking the Reader's head with a hand.

"Talk is all I have," replied the Reader. "So you must listen. The fated three are finally gathered: the warrior, the ruler and the witch. Jonas is Thom's successor. Lana Shadowscale is the ruler, who can lead both humans and Kind. And you – my feathered friend – you are the *wizard* who will stand at her side." She coughed, and more blood spilt from her lips. "I know I tease you, but I see it now." She gasped in pain, tensing up. "You three can bring about the Cleansing. Finally, the peace of

Havanthya can return. Peace for all its people."

And with those words, Jonas felt death sweep past and snatch the Reader's spirit. Her eyes stopped moving and her body sagged.

"She's gone," said Alia.

18

THE LAST STAND

"*Y*ou have to help her," Jun begged Gael. "Without our leader, we have no chance! The troops will lose heart and the defences will crumble!"

"I cannot restore the dead to life," said Gael sadly. "Our only hope now is that the Empress's army will break the siege in time."

Lana felt the attention of everyone present settle on to her.

This wasn't the scene Gael had prepared her for. The Reader who'd marshalled the rebels lay dead before her. The city was on the brink of being overrun. Lana had little time to dwell on what the Reader had said about the Cleansing. Prophecies were all well and good, but they didn't win battles.

"Take me to the forest," Lana told Gael. "Jonas," she added to the boy with the golden breastplate. "Keep Resala's forces occupied with the phoenix. I'll lead my troops to attack them from the rear."

"Very well." Jonas nodded. "Halima, stay here, out of harm's way."

The human girl shook her head. "No, my place is with my people." With that, she turned and sprinted for the door.

Gael came to Lana's side, holding the purple jewel. "Are you ready, Empress?"

Lana nodded and took Jun's hand. In the blink of an eye they were at the forest's edge, where soldiers filled the spaces between the trees. The first rank were made up of the Empress's Own, drawn up in their resplendent uniforms and holding redsteel spears. Behind them were more heavily armoured lizard-Kind infantry, many bearing the heraldic crests of Whitestone's aristocratic families and armed with heavy swords. Last of all, hovering or perched in the branches, were bird-Kind in light leather armour. These troops carried crossbows.

Gael disappeared again just as the soldiers noticed their Empress. At the sight of her, they stood up straighter. She raised a hand for silence and spoke as loudly and forcefully as she could.

"Today we fight against those who would destroy us and plunge the Four Kingdoms into eternal conflict," she called. "It matters not whether they are human or Kind. Since the Spawning, and indeed before, this land has known only distrust and conflict. Today we have a chance to end that and set our lives – all lives – on a new path of peace." She turned and pointed to the walls of the Lost City, where Aephos was circling.

"The old-Kind are waking," she cried. "They have seen the long arc of our history. They know the cost of conflict, but they also remember what can be bought with it. So today I ask you all to pay that price with blood and courage. To drive our enemies from the field. To put your faith in me, your Empress, to deliver the freedom and prosperity of a new golden age. Will you follow me into battle?"

The assembled troops shouted, stamping their feet and banging their weapons. At Lana's side, even Jun looked on at her in awe.

Lana pointed towards the city walls, where insect-Kind and Resala's human armies were rallying.

"Then attack! In the name of peace, of justice and of New Havanthya!"

The armies charged past her, through the air and

across the ground, swarming towards the enemy. Resala's tribesfolk blared trumpets to alert their troops to the rear-guard action. Half their forces detached from the assault on the city to deal with this new attack. Lana was about to join the advance, when she saw two unlikely figures approaching from the forest.

Uncle Bart had squeezed into his ceremonial armour, and at his side was Shahn.

Lana's immediate surprise quickly turned to anger.

"What are you doing here?" she asked.

"Shahn insisted!" said Bart, puffing hard.

"You know how stubborn these Shadowscale girls can be," said Jun.

"I wanted to see you use your magic," said Shahn, meeting Lana's eyes. "You're always trying to keep me out of things!"

"For good reason," said Lana. "This is a battlefield." She gestured to the sky, where the bird-Kind were engaging in the air with Resala's flying beetles. Bodies clashed and corpses began to fall to the ground just ahead of where they stood. "I can't fight *and* keep you safe. Stay here. And, Uncle – show some backbone! Don't let her get any closer."

With that admonishment, she ran towards the battle.

Redsteel-armed tribesfolk with painted skin saw her coming and rushed towards her. Lana met them with her shadow powers. She seized great clods of earth and hurled them at the attackers, smashing them aside or burying them under tons of rubble. To wield the elements, all she need do was reach for them. She felt unstoppable.

Though she was sure she could keep herself safe, the rest of her armies were in peril. A detachment of heavily armed warriors had appeared on their flanks, their redsteel armour proclaiming their allegiance to Resala and Florenz. The first wave of them were galloping bear- and wolf-Kind, who crashed with all their might and speed into the Empress's Own. Next came elk- and ox-Kind, mercenaries from the far and frozen north. Though Lana's bird-Kind peppered them from above with crossbows, their missiles were no match for redsteel armour. The beetle-Kind leading the attack on the walls broke away and came back to help too. Aephos followed them, knocking those she could from the sky, but others clamped on to her wings in an effort to bring her down. High above, Lana saw Jonas on the firebird's back, slashing at the attackers with his scimitar blades.

It wouldn't be enough, she realised. The numbers were simply against them.

That left just one other option. A dangerous one, but perhaps the only way to prevent countless deaths and unnecessary bloodshed. She would need to exercise the full power she had tasted in the chamber of the Mothers of Fate.

Slowing her steps, Lana glanced back to check on Shahn. Her sister was still under the trees with Bart and Jun, avidly watching the battle. Lana lifted her hands, invoking the runes from the Tablets of the Creator as she'd done before. Her shadow surged, like fire caught in a gust of wind.

"What are you doing?" asked Gael.

The old crow really did come and go as he pleased.

"Whatever I can," replied Lana.

A gateway to the Netherplane appeared in front of her. The portal opened more easily this time, as easily as opening the door to another room. Though this was a door through which she'd peered once before, she still wondered what she would find on the other side. The lure of the Netherplane's magic was powerful and tempting, but was it truly under her control or would it overwhelm her like it had her mother, scouring her brain of sanity?

"I don't think this is a good idea," muttered Gael.

Lana had no other choice. Only a demonstration of ultimate power could end this battle.

With her will alone, she pulled raw magic from the Netherplane, absorbing it into her body and then casting it out over the heads of the armies. Above the battlefield, Aephos let out a keening cry as she wheeled away from the crest of terrible power.

The black cloud of shadow coalesced, like the falling of a sudden storm. In its depths, Lana shaped the magic into the forms of the great old-Kind Elementals of the past – Fernwing, Sephron and the other creatures of lore she'd seen the Creator summon to the shores of the lake under Whitestone. Their bodies writhed and pounced, scattering Resala's armies, turning them from fearsome fighters to terrified children in a moment.

When Lana spoke, the colossal beings amplified her voice in a booming wave that made the walls tremble and every living thing cower.

"You cannot resist the Creator's heir," she cried. "Witness the power of Lana Shadowscale!"

Even Gael looked on in astonishment.

Lana drew the magic to her again. She willed the elemental forms into a gale of spectral essence and sent it whipping through the edge of the forest, stripping the trees of their leaves. Howls of dismay and fear passed through Resala's forces there, and they began to toss their weapons to the ground. Lana hurled the magic across the battlefield again, letting them feel the weight of her power, snatching up siege engines, ladders and towers and shattering them against the ground, smashing them to splinters. Now even the most stout-hearted of fighters surrendered, some lying prostrate as well, or even offering up begging prayers.

For a moment there was silence. On the walls, the rebel defenders looked on in awe. Aephos had landed, and Jonas sat on her back. He looked as mesmerised as everyone else. Lana stood wreathed in her power, imperious and undaunted.

Now they know what I can do, she thought. *They're in my palm.*

But a cry of alarm caught her attention. There, at the forest's edge, stood Kezia. To Lana's horror, the renegade sorceress held a struggling Shahn. One arm was wrapped around the girl's neck and another circled her middle. Bart and Jun lay on the ground nearby, moaning weakly.

"Let her go!" shouted Lana, running forward. As her voice rose, she felt the magic respond, the shadow around her forming angry spikes. Kezia must have seen this too, though she only smiled.

"You betrayed Malachai," she spat back. "You were working against the Order of the True from the beginning. You won't get away with it, *Empress*."

"Kezia, whatever you're planning, don't," said Gael. "The battle is over. You have lost."

"Yet the war continues," said Kezia. Her yellow wolf-eyes flashed in fury. "For every crime, there comes a price. And this is hers." Though the sorceress appeared unarmed, Kezia leaned close to Shahn's ear to whisper something.

The effect was immediate – Shahn glanced up at her sister, a look of confusion crossing her face, as though she'd heard something no child should. Something she didn't quite understand, but which terrified her nonetheless. Then her eyes rolled back in her head, and she fell limply to the ground.

"Shahn!" screamed Lana.

Kezia stepped back as Bart scrambled to his niece's side, feeling for a pulse.

"She's . . . dead!" he wailed.

"A death-curse will have that effect," said Kezia.

"She was innocent!" cried Gael. "You monster!"

Lana fell to her knees at Shahn's side and rolled her sister over. Her eyes were still completely white, and no breath escaped her lips. With a dawning horror, she remembered the Creator's words. *The sacrifice must have my blood.*

Was this what he had meant? If Shahn too shared the blood of the Creator, was her life the price of the Cleansing?

"Wake up," muttered Lana, shaking her sister gently. Shahn didn't react at all. Her skin already felt cold. She looked up at Kezia. "Undo the curse!" she said. "Or I *will* kill you."

The sorceress trembled and stepped back further, yet she remained defiant. "You should never have brought her to Whitestone, Lana Shadowscale. Her death is your doing."

Lana laid her sister down gently and rose to her feet. "Bring her back or I will kill you, witch."

Kezia shook her head firmly. "You must learn humility, upstart," she said. "Let this be my lesson to you. You think you will keep your throne now they have seen what you truly are? You're not an empress, you're a monster."

"You dare call me a monster when you've killed the sweetest, most dear—"

Lana broke off what she was saying as pain shot through her temples. She felt the magical energy around her boil and froth, escaping the bounds of her power. She struggled to hold it, to control it, to shape it, but with her fury it redoubled. The ground at her feet shook, and Kezia's eyes widened. "What are you doing?"

The forests and fields gave a sudden lurch.

Gael's beak was hanging open as he crouched beside Shahn. Even Lana did not know what was going on. She wasn't *doing* anything. The quake was happening by itself. Above her, the black shadow magic she'd brought from the Netherplane churned like a tornado, thickening and darkening into a disc of pure malevolent energy.

She tried to make it dissipate but it wouldn't. She was the conduit for its power, but it was out of her control. The mass of shadow swelled, releasing a tendril that extended towards Kezia. The sorceress stumbled backwards and fell, shielding herself with her arms and crying out in fear. As the shadow touched her, the cry became a scream of pain as her skin turned grey, then black, then began to flake away like ash. In a matter of seconds, her body had crumbled to dust.

With an ominous silence, more tendrils extended across the battlefield, searching for prey. Gael took Shahn's limp body and vanished in a flash. As the magic tentacles touched the defenceless soldiers – Kind and humans alike, rebel and tribesman and imperial soldier – each one disintegrated in an instant just like Kezia had done. Some ran but didn't get far before the magic reached them. Others tried to shrink away and hide, ending their lives curled into foetal balls. The beetle-Kind who took to the air couldn't escape it either. The ash of their remains rained down on the fields.

Lana knew it was only a matter of time before the dark magic reached the walls, and it would be the city's occupants who died next.

"No," said Lana. "I don't want this . . ."

Make it stop! she willed.

But it didn't. It was beyond her control, a power unto itself, released from the Netherplane and greedy for slaughter.

She was as helpless before the terrible force as everyone else.

19

THE CLEANSING

From the city's walls, Jonas looked upon the carnage spreading below. The armies were turning to dust before his eyes. A power had entered their world that had no place here. It was pure malice and murder.

"You need to stop her," said Gael as he appeared suddenly next to Jonas. "She's lost control." In his arms, Gael held the body of Lana's sister, recovered from the forest's edge.

"How can I stop this?" said Jonas. "Isn't this the Cleansing? Isn't this what you wanted?"

"I didn't want *this*," Gael said.

A tendril of the deathly shadow magic snaked towards them. Gael gently laid Shahn's body on the ground, then spread a hand against the encroaching tendril. It shrank back, as if stung. "This is not the true Cleansing – it's a massacre. Lana's despair has unleashed something she cannot control, and now her sister is dead. If we don't stop it, all living things will die."

In time, all living things do die, thought Jonas. *Maybe it's our time.*

But in the same moment, an idea hit him. It was true that death came for everyone, but not all remained dead.

"Aephos!" he said. "Can you use *your* life force to save Lana's sister?"

Beside him, Gael jerked his head around. "*What?*"

Jonas faced the old crow earnestly. "If we can bring her sister back, Lana might regain the control she's lost."

"Shahn's gone." Gael shook his head. "A tragic, senseless loss, but she's just a girl. We *need* Aephos to stop Vedrios." He extended his other arm, holding at bay more of the shadow tendrils threatening to sneak into the city. "I can't hold these back for long. There are too many."

"She's just a girl to you," said Jonas. "But to Lana, she's everything."

You wish me to sacrifice myself for this girl, and

not to use my life to rid you of your death-blessing? asked Aephos.

"I do."

It will be many years before I can rise again from the ashes. You will live with your own corruption until the end of your days. Consider wisely.

Jonas already had. He'd lived with the spirit of Krimios lurking in his heart for his whole life. In that time, he'd witnessed, or taken part in, the slaughter of hundreds. Shahn Shadowscale was the first he'd ever been able to bring back. By doing so, there was a chance of saving countless more lives.

"Do it, *please!*" he said. "And thank you, Aephos."

As you wish, Master of the Kind.

The giant phoenix lowered her head and touched Shahn's scaled forehead with her beak. For a moment, it glowed like polished gold, before the light seemed to pass from the old-Kind to the girl. A last ripple of fire flickered over the flame bird's feathers. As the flame died, the feathers disintegrated. Aephos shrank before their eyes, breaking apart like the embers of a burned-out cooking fire. Her tail was first to crumble, then her wings, and finally her neck and head. Jonas held the mighty bird's gaze until that too vanished, and all that remained of her was a pall of smoke.

"Has it worked?" asked Gael. He was focused on protecting them and the city from the tendrils of shadow, but risked a peek over his shoulder.

Jonas looked closer at the girl on the ground, willing her to show a sign of life. Then Shahn stirred, her eyes fluttering open. "What happened?" she asked.

"Several things," said Gael. His legs trembled as he held the deadly magic off. "Most of them quite horrible, but you've been given a second chance at life, so I suppose that's something. Now we just need to let your sister know before she kills us and every other being in the Four Kingdoms."

Jonas tried shouting to Lana. But the distance between them was vast and his voice was lost in the roar of the magical energies she'd summoned.

Shahn joined in, yelling her sister's name until she was hoarse. "She can't hear us!"

Gael staggered under the burden of his wards as his knees gave way. "Then we will all die," he said. "I cannot transport you any closer. If I do, these tendrils will strike the city and thousands more will perish."

Jonas looked out across the battlefield. The deadly

magic swirled in all directions. There was no way to reach Lana.

Unless . . .

"Gael, is it true that the element of ghost is resistant to magic?"

The crow-Kind nodded. "Yes, ghost is a non-physical element, so magic can pass right through it but . . ." His eyes widened. "Jonas, you *can't*!"

"I must," said Jonas. "It's our only chance."

He closed his eyes and tried to remember the feeling among the bleeding trees of the Forbidden Lands, and the very moment when the spirit of Krimios had taken over his body. Could he do it again? Did he dare to allow the malevolent essence out? And if he did, could he control it?

There's no other way.

Almost at once, he felt the surge of Krimios's presence across his chest, powerful and enticing. It swelled against the confines of the golden breastplate.

"Come, Krimios," he mumbled.

Images flashed through his mind: of distant lands; of flying beside his brother Vedrios; of his own tribe falling before his claws. Of the shamans' chant before the sangwar roots, calling to him. The memories surged and merged.

Jonas reached out his arms to see them thicken, growing a coating of red scales. He saw his face extend into a snout and felt his spine stretch and realign. He sensed the weight and power of his wings as they obeyed his commands and flapped at his sides, gauging their strength.

Shahn had backed right away, terrified at his transformation. Gael too was shaking his head, as though he couldn't believe what he was seeing.

Jonas turned to where Lana stood, her body stiff amid the raw and roiling magic that poured from the portal like water through a breached dam. The shifting shadows were no threat to him now, so Jonas leapt from the walls and let the wind fill his wings. Gliding across the fallen troops, he landed at Lana's side.

"You have to stop this!" he shouted over the storm. His voice was deeper and rougher. Jonas was transformed, but the golden breastplate kept Krimios from gaining full control.

Lana turned a desperate gaze towards him, her eyes quickly drawn to the golden breastplate. "Is that you, Jonas? I can't stop it!" she said. "It's too much!"

"You'll kill everyone," said Jonas. "You know you don't want that."

"No," Lana said, but then her gaze seemed to cloud. "But then, why should I care? My sister is dead. They can all die too."

"She's alive!" said Jonas. "*Look!*" He extended a wing to the walls, where Shahn now stood with Gael. Even more shadows reached for them now, inching ever closer.

"Shahn . . . ?" said Lana. "But I saw her die."

"The phoenix Aephos brought her back," said Jonas. "Now stop this, please!"

Lana's eyes held the briefest glimmer of hope before her face hardened. "It's too late. I can't control it. The magic has taken over." Then her features tightened and she said, "The *Cleansing* is coming!"

Saying this, her voice boomed deeply, as though it belonged to a darker power working through her. Perhaps he wasn't the only one battling an inner demon.

"No!" yelled Jonas, squinting into the portal. "Lana, *listen*. The Reader put her trust in us. Don't let her sacrifice be in vain. You alone have the power to bring peace. That's what you want. For your sister – for everyone!"

When he saw her features twist, he knew he was getting through to her. "I . . . can't!" she pleaded.

"It's too much."

"Close the portal!" he said. "There must be a way."

Lana reached slowly towards the folds of her cloak, fingers trembling as if fighting through a hidden forcefield. She retrieved a white jewel from her pocket. Her whole body shook as she held it to her chest, teeth gritted. As she did so, the shadows lurched away from her. Jonas didn't understand what was happening, but he could see the mighty struggle she was going through. Her edges blurred, as if her very form was breaking apart, and very slowly, the shadow that clung to her lifted away, forming a second Lana at her side – a dark twin birthed from her body. In the air, the maelstrom of shadow screamed as though in pain.

The shadow Lana took faltering steps towards the portal, leaving her bodily version behind holding the white crystal. As Jonas watched, willing her on, the shadow figure forced itself against an invisible wind, until it reached the portal's edge. The Lana who was flesh had set her jaw, as her eyes blazed fiercely at her counterpart. The shadow leapt through the portal. In the same moment, all of the licking tendrils fled from the sky.

The terrible disc of magical energies was sucked

through the portal with a roar. When its last shreds departed, the portal blinked out of existence.

Eerie silence fell over the broken walls of the Lost City and Lana Shadowscale collapsed to the ground in a limp heap.

20

THE ENCHANTER

At first Jonas thought she was dead.

His heart lifted as she slowly rolled to one side. When she opened her eyes, there was something different about Lana Shadowscale.

"My shadow . . ." she said as she sat up and gazed at her body. "It's gone!"

In the next moment, Gael and Shahn appeared next to them. Lana's little sister rushed in for an embrace.

"You did it," said Gael, voice filled with pride. "You fought back against the magic and prevailed."

"My powers are gone," said Lana. She inspected her arm, then glanced at Gael. "For ever?"

Gael beamed. "The white jewel allowed you

to send your magical self to the Netherplane. A sacrifice worthy of an empress."

Shahn, still in her sister's arms, suddenly looked across at Jonas with eyes wide. "Look out!"

Jonas felt spikes of pain across his shoulders as the force of a great weight knocked him forward. As he fell, the golden breastplate dropped away from his chest, its straps sliced through. The form of Krimios shone more brightly across his body, and with it came a surge of bloodlust.

In an instant, the thirst for slaughter took him completely.

Seth stood behind him. "*There* you are, brother."

The words resonated deep within Jonas, in the part of him that was alien and always hungry for slaughter. His lips formed words of their own accord. When he spoke, it was with a dragon's rasp. "Vedrios, my dear twin," he replied.

"Time for our vengeance," said his wyvern brother. "Time to kill."

Jonas fought back, forcing his voice past that of the red dragon who was becoming ever more present inside him. "Kill *who*?"

"All of them," said Seth calmly. "The Empress, the wizard, the girl. All the humans of this city. Kill them just as you've killed so many before."

The frightening thing was that Jonas *wanted* to. Though he remembered these people were his allies, his talons and teeth sought flesh and warm blood. He imagined the sheer, unbridled joy of ripping his tribe to pieces and exulting in his old-Kind power. His true nature had been leashed for long enough. Now was the time to be free. Now was the time to *feed*.

"Remember yourself!" implored Gael. "You are Jonas, not Krimios, and you are the fated Master of the Kind. You are chosen."

"*Chosen?*" sneered Seth. "You haven't the power to decide fate, crow. The boy is nothing but a vessel for my brother's spirit. The fire of a dragon cannot be quenched . . ."

He's right. I feel it, burning brightly. Ready to consume.

"He's been chosen by Thom himself," continued Gael. "Chosen to walk the Master's Road. Chosen to unite the Kind and humans."

"And what makes you think he's worthy of such things?" said Seth. "You should have listened to the Reader, because she was right about this at least. If you think this *boy* is your saviour, you've chosen your champion poorly. Without me to hold his hand and save his skin, he's a weakling and a

250

coward. He always has been."

I am weak. *I am* cursed. *But I can leave all that behind and become something new.*

"You lie," said Gael. "Without you he has slain Grashkor, tamed Moonfear and even won over Aephos. He need but defeat one more old-Kind before he takes his rightful place as Thom's heir. I see now what he must do. It's been obvious from the start. He must kill *you*."

Seth laughed. "Me? You're dreaming, sorcerer. Krimios is my brother hatchling. We are bonded by old-Kind blood." He looked at Jonas. "Come now, Krimios, show them who you are. Give rein to your anger and sink your teeth into their soft hearts."

Jonas felt himself – his soul – dangling by its fingertips, clinging on to . . . something. What was it – *himself*? His past? It would be so much easier simply to let go and let his wings unfurl. To leave it in the past and embrace the new. No guilt. No pain. Just flight, and feasting, and the glory of his form. With his brother at his side, they would be unstoppable. They would repay the wrongs done to their Kind, to *all* Kind.

We will cleanse this world of Humanity!

He saw Seth's green heart pulse in his chest, while his own huge red heart beat in the same rhythm.

And yet. And yet . . . this wasn't really his heart. This powerful crimson centre belonged to Krimios. But it wasn't alone. Peering into his ghostly form, Jonas saw that another heart throbbed beside it. A human one, weak as the fluttering of a bird's, pumping the same blood that had flowed through Fran's veins, and his mother's and his father's.

He was Krimios but he was also still Jonas.

"No," Jonas said firmly.

He sensed Krimios's spirit shrink away a little, though he remained in his scaled and winged form. He reached back to draw both weapons, the Swords of What Was and What Will Be. He crossed them in front of his chest. "You are not welcome in this world, Vedrios. One way or another, let's end this. Fight me if you must."

The vicious smile on Seth's lips faded and became a sneer. "Very well, *human*. But you'll have to catch me first."

He spun and flew away towards the bare forest.

"It's a trick!" said Gael. "Don't!"

But Jonas was already airborne on Krimios's wings, flying after Seth. His brother was quicker and more adept in the air, flitting between the trees. Jonas followed, not quite so nimble. Shifting into a human form, he crashed through the branches and bounced off the trunks. But he didn't let these minor knocks stop him. Without the golden breastplate, his death-song was building. He longed to finish Seth for good – to hack him to pieces if he needed to.

That's right, Little Fury. Let me guide you.

The voice came not from his mouth, but the red glow in his chest.

"Who are you?" said Jonas, though he already knew the answer.

I am Krimios. I am you.

Jonas couldn't see Seth ahead, but suddenly the wyvern stepped out from behind a tree, swinging a branch that caught Jonas in the middle and knocked him to the ground. Caught off guard, fighting for his breath, Jonas was confused. Why hadn't his death-song shown him the threat?

Seth stepped in front of Jonas, throwing down the branch. "When I kill you, my brother will consume your life force. He's strong enough now. Finally, he'll be complete once again."

Jonas saw his death. *Seth pounces and with a single flick of his claws cuts through Jonas's neck. Blood spills in a torrent over his chest.*

By instinct, Jonas ducked, but the attack never came. He launched himself at Seth, hoping to pin him down, but he landed on empty air and sprawled.

"Still trusting the death-song?" Seth laughed, suddenly behind him. "Old habits die hard, I suppose."

Seth slices and a claw rips open Jonas's guts.

Jonas threw up his blade to deflect, but Seth instead stabbed low, cutting deep into his thigh.

The death-song wasn't working, Jonas realised. He couldn't trust it any more.

Because I am your death-song, said Krimios. *I sing what I like.*

Jonas staggered away, trying to ignore the pain and work out what to do. The defence he'd relied on all his life was failing. Krimios and Vedrios were working together.

"It could have been so different," taunted Seth. "If only you'd given yourself willingly. We could have been brothers for ever."

"I'd rather die," said Jonas through gritted teeth. His blood spattered the leaf litter.

Seth cackled. "Yes, that's the idea," he said. He slashed again, catching Jonas's wrist. Pain seared up his arm. "I'll slice you up, piece by piece, until all that remains is my true brother."

I'm waiting, Vedrios, said Krimios inside Jonas's head. *Free me from this prison of useless flesh.*

Jonas felt another stinging blow across his back and dropped to the ground. Hand over hand, he crawled.

"Don't run away, brother," Seth taunted. Looking back, Jonas saw Seth following on foot, as if he had all the time in the world.

Then, through the trees, Jonas saw her: Fran.

"You have to let go, Jonas," said Fran. "Close your ears to the past. To the death-song. Leave What Was behind. Leave your guilt. Leave us."

Behind, Jonas saw other figures, cast in shadow. He knew they were his tribe. Or at least their ghosts.

Fran reached out to him with a delicate hand. "Leave me."

"I can't fail you again," said Jonas. "I killed you. All of you."

"It wasn't you," said Fran. "It was never you."

It was us, said Krimios's voice. *What you let yourself become, and what you will be again.*

The tribesfolk disappeared in the shadows, but Fran remained, keeping pace as Jonas dragged himself across the forest floor. Seth came after him, clearly enjoying the chase. "Stop fighting, Jonas," he said. "You've been fighting all your life."

"You can be who you were before," said Fran. "Thom recognised your goodness, but *you* have to do so as well. You can be the Master, not the Slayer. You can stand at the side of the Empress, as friend to the Kind and protector of Havanthya."

Jonas pulled himself upright against the trunk of a tree. He stumbled to the next one. Where he was running to, he didn't know. Seth could strike him down at any moment. And while Seth was in ghost-form, no weapon could harm him. If Jonas could land a strike when Seth was solid, he might have a chance, but that would involve speed and surprise. As his blood leaked away, Jonas knew he had neither.

He fell against another tree, and this one gave a little, its immense trunk rotten at the base and sprouting grey fungus. Jonas had a flash of memory from his boyhood: he walked beside his father through a deep forest to gather firewood. He remembered marvelling at the size of the axe his father carried with so little effort. Such rotted trees were ripe for firewood, easy to fell, he heard his father say. The trick was to cut the trunk so you could direct the fall.

That was the past, of course, before he'd cut his father down along with the others. But it gave him the spark of an idea.

"Enough of this," said Seth. "Give in, Jonas, and

I will make it quick."

Jonas spun around with a wild slash of the Sword of What Was. As he expected, Seth dodged easily, the sword passing through his ghostly body. The blade bit deep into the soft trunk. Jonas tried to tug it free, but Seth shot forward, suddenly solid, and punched him in the chest. Jonas tripped over a root and fell backwards.

"Now, that wasn't nice!" said Seth. "After all I've done for you."

"You've ruined my life," said Jonas. "Everything you did was deceit."

"I did it for my brother," said Seth. "What we do for family, right?"

Jonas peered past him. Fran was gone, but the Sword of What Was remained lodged in the tree, quivering. The rotted trunk teetered, ready to fall.

Jonas was back in the forest of his youth again, with his father.

Stand back, son. She's going to come down any second. It'll only take a push.

Jonas drew his remaining sword, pointing it at Seth.

"Come on, then, Little Fury," said the wyvern, his ghostly form shimmering as he spread his wings. "Time for one last *brave* stand."

Jonas hurled the blade, sending it spinning through the air. It passed through Seth's ghostly form to hit the half-felled tree.

"Do it!" bellowed Jonas. "Kill me if you even have the mettle for it!"

Seth pounced quickly, and his claws – now solid and powerful – were around Jonas's throat in an instant. He hoisted him into the air and squeezed, all the while staring into Jonas's eyes.

"I see you in there, Krimios," he hissed. "Take this life force and make it yours. Steal his last breath and make it your first for a thousand years."

Jonas held Vedrios's emerald gaze, drinking in his hatred. Why had he never seen it before, in all their time together? How could he have been so blind to Seth's true motives? He gripped Seth's shoulder with his own hand, reassured that it was solid. In his peripheral vision, he sensed the shadow of the falling trunk. Only at the creak of the splintering wood did Seth turn to look. The wyvern enjoyed no death-song. He didn't see it coming until it was too late.

He was too busy trying to end Jonas's life to protect his own.

His claws loosened, and Jonas used the last of his strength to leap aside. The colossal trunk crashed down, hitting Seth with a thump and crushing him beneath it.

Jonas picked himself up and edged closer. He could hear breathing, but it was shallow and laboured. A rattle. He saw one wing, broken and splayed at an angle, and then the rest of the wyvern, pinned down by the trunk that had destroyed his torso. One eye was shot through with blood, and his lips were moving, not with words but grimaces of pain.

Jonas looked down at his own chest, but there was no longer any sign of Krimios's ghostly glow now.

The only heart that beat in Jonas's chest was his own.

Seth's one good eye came to rest on him, and the wyvern managed the briefest smile. "My Little Fury," he mumbled.

And then the tree shifted as the body beneath it seemed to melt away into pure ghostly essence. Seth was gone. And Jonas felt in his core that it was for good this time.

Jonas felt unburdened. He could not remember ever feeling so light. The death-song fell silent in his heart; his long curse was lifted.

He was free.

21

NEW HAVANTHYA

"**F**arewell, dear friend," muttered Gael under his breath as he looked upwards.

The Reader's statue was one of three new monuments erected before the White Palace. Without Lana's shadow-blessed skills, Gael had been worried the workmanship might falter in comparison to the depictions of Elrith and the former Emperor, but he was rather pleased with the results. The finest craftsmen had been drafted in from all corners of the Four Kingdoms and worked day and night to complete the assignment.

Roshni stood in a simple pose, hands clasped, calmly surveying the central square with a wise gaze. The artist had even captured the hint of a smile tugging at the corner of her lips, as it had so often when she was alive. Some had suggested interring the rebel leader in the Gallery of Tombs, but Gael knew that his friend Roshni would have hated that. So instead, once her body had been retrieved and shrouded for burial, he'd transported her back to the mountains where she'd been born – to her people.

Over the course of his long life, Gael had witnessed countless human deaths, but hers had hit him hard. He'd miss her terribly, especially their good-hearted sparring, but he consoled himself that her dream of peace had come to pass.

Beside the Reader's statue was one of Jonas, sitting astride Aephos, wielding his swords as he had done in the battle for the Lost City. Gael wondered if he'd ever live to see the rebirth of the great phoenix again.

The next of the new statues was Dalthek himself, holding his gnarled wooden staff.

Lana had wanted more humans represented among these great statues in Whitestone, and so she had chosen this celebrated human wizard of yore.

Here before the palace, these three marble figures stood in all their grandeur. Three protectors –

Leader, Warrior and Wizard – symbolising for all the new peace.

In the square, the gathered humans and Kind stood mostly apart. Gael guessed it would be some time before old habits died. But here and there he was heartened to see a little mixing. Lana Shadowscale had instituted a special committee to oversee the reconciliation. She had already overturned the old rules that prohibited humans owning property in the city or being members of the various trade guilds. Before the Empress's dais, her personal guards were a symbol of New Havanthya. The Empress's Own were now a combination of lizard-Kind and humans. These were former rebels from the Lost City who had taken vows in support of the lizard-Kind leader who'd come to their aid against Resala's armies. Alia, their new captain, watched on with a severe expression, alert to any threats.

It would take many such gestures for the old wounds to truly heal.

The Empress herself sat on her throne, with Jun standing a few paces behind her. Lana's shadow had been gone since the day of the battle, and with it her magic-blessing. It had returned to the Netherplane where it had come from in the first place. Maybe that was for the best, thought Gael.

Too much power always corrupted in the end.

At Lana's side stood Jonas, resplendent – though looking a little uncomfortable – in newly forged golden armour. Gael allowed himself a smile of pride at the part he'd played in the boy's journey. Orphan to Slayer to Master of the Kind. Lana had commissioned an official songwriter to compose an account of his epic deeds, and the comparison was already being made with the famous Masters of yore – Thaladon, Thom and Thanner.

"Is it true that you're a thousand years old?" asked a small voice.

Gael looked down and saw the young sister of Lana, wearing what looked like a new dress made of Red Isle silk. A portly man hurried up behind her.

"Now, Shahn, no interrupting." He glanced at Gael. "My apologies – she's always wandering off."

"It's quite all right," said Gael. He kneeled down beside the girl. "Actually, I'm not sure of my exact age. We don't celebrate birthdays in the Netherplane."

"Well, I'm twelve in a month," said Shahn. "And for my birthday I've asked for a redsteel dagger."

"Have you? And what will you do with that?"

Shahn put her hands on her hips. "Be a warrior, of course! To protect my sister."

Gael smiled as he straightened up. "I'm sure you will."

"Make way! Make way!" shouted a member of the Empress's Own. A column of soldiers pressed through the crowd towards them. When they arrived, the commander at the fore said to Gael, "Her Highness would like a word, if you don't mind?"

Gael followed them back to the stage, climbing up beside Lana's throne.

"You summoned me?" he said with a bow.

"I suppose I did," said Lana. "It's rather nice when everyone does as you ask. I wanted to know why you lied to me."

Gael put a hand to his chest. "Me? Your Highness, I assure you, I've always told you the truth."

Lana grinned. "Not about my father."

Gael kept a straight face. "I'm not sure I follow your meaning."

Lana turned and pointed to the statue of Dalthek. "That forked staff," she said. "It's based on the description from the *Chronicles of Havanthya*. It's also exactly the same as the one I saw in the hands of the Creator in the Netherplane. Which makes me think . . ."

"Yes?" said Gael innocently.

"Well, that perhaps Dalthek *was* the Creator, all this time."

Gael cocked his head. "That would be a theory for the scholars, not an old crow like me."

". . . *and*," continued Lana, "that would mean Dalthek was actually my father."

In truth, Gael had worked this out himself some time ago. "I shouldn't think about it too hard," he said. "You have Four Kingdoms to run now. Plenty of enemies to worry about."

Behind the throne, Jun cleared her throat. "He's right, Your Highness. The scouts still haven't found either Kezia or Resala. It's believed they could be in the mountains, perhaps even working together. Some of the Kind long for how things were before. The old Emperor seems content in his retirement, but should Malachai ever awaken, he could rally many under his banner."

"There's also Silash and Florenz," added Jonas. "They may be in prison, but they still have droves of supporters."

"It's lucky I have a Master of the Kind at my side, then," said Lana. "Keep your swords sharp, Jonas. I fear they will be needed soon."

"While the Masters' blood pumps through my veins," said Jonas, "I serve at your pleasure."

Gael turned and squinted at the sun reflecting off Whitestone's walls, and then at the myriad Kind and humans gathered below. Fragile harmony reigned in the Four Kingdoms, with the promise, under Lana Shadowscale and her allies, of a long peace. But if there was one thing Gael's centuries among the mortals had taught him, it was that evil could never be stamped out completely. Somewhere, enemies were already scheming.

But they would be ready.